HOLY SATURDAY

AND

OTHER STORIES

EZEQUIEL MARTINEZ ESTRADA

TRANSLATED BY

LELAND H. CHAMBERS

LATIN AMERICAN LITERARY REVIEW PRESS
SERIES: DISCOVERIES
PITTSBURGH, PENNSYLVANIA

YVETTE E. MILLER, EDITOR

1988

The Latin American Literary Review Press publishes Latin American creative writing under the series title *Discoveries*, and critical works under the series title *Explorations*.

Translation   1988 Leland H. Chambers and Latin American Literary Review Press

Library of Congress Cataloging-in-Publication Data

Martínez Estrada, Ezequiel, 1895-1964.
  Holy Saturday and other stories.

  (Discoveries)
  Contents: Holy Saturday -- Marta Riquelme --
  Examination Without Honor -- The Deluge
  I. Title. II. Series
PQ7797.M277A24 1988   863   88-12760
ISBN 0-935480-30-7

Cover by Lisette D. Miller

Holy Saturday and Other Stories can be ordered directly from the publisher:

Latin American Literary Review Press
2300 Palmer Street
Pittsburgh,Pennsylvania 15218

Table of Contents

This project is supported by grants from the National Endowment for the Arts in Washington, D.C., a Federal Agency, the Commonwealth of Pennsylvania Council on the Arts, and the University of Denver.

INTRODUCTION

BY

PETER G. EARLE

Martínez Estrada's stories are best described as nightmares. They reflect hidden desires and everyday frustrations; they're rooted in inexplicable dilemmas; their endings allow for no solution. Like the extensive essays for which he's better known (*X-Ray of the Pampa*, 1933; *The Head of Goliath*, 1940; *Sarmiento*, 1946; *Death and Transfiguration of Martín Fierro*, 1948; *The Marvelous World of William Henry Hudson*, 1951), the author's short fiction repeatedly recalls the fate of Prometheus, the West's first dramatization of human failure and suffering.

Prometheus seems to have been the archetype, in essays as well as in fiction, for most of this Argentine writer's protagonists; the gaucho as a perennial social outcast; the frustrated office worker or ingenuous hospital patient as existential victim; the sensitive young woman, in Carl Gustav Jung's words, as "an indefiniteness that seems full of promises, like the speaking silence of a Mona Lisa."

Born in a small country town in the province of Buenos Aires in 1895, Martínez Estrada came to the city when he was twenty-one; he was never to feel quite at home there. The Head of Goliath is his metaphor for Buenos Aires, the sprawling capital city which, he contends, lives at the expense of the rest of the country. It impressed him as an alien place, and it is no accident that it became the central symbol for three of the four stories included in this volume. In 1945 Victoria Ocampo asked him to write an autobiographical letter for publication in her prestigious literary journal, *Sur*. In it he confesses his despondent conviction that "to prolong life beyond puberty is a fatal error that one pays for with survival itself" and, further, that he remembers no time in his life in which he was able "to experience a child's innocence." William Henry Hudson, who grew up on the Argentine pampas and for whom nature, beauty and virtue formed an indivisible trinity, and Friedrich Nietzsche, who wrote always as the rebel prophet, were his favorite authors.

The letter to Victoria Ocampo is basically confessional—in tone and attitude—though never in specific detail. From the testimony of several others we know that the author of *X-Ray of the Pampas* led quite a stark existence (one acquaintance, Rafael Alberto Arrieta, writes that in the 1920's Martínez

Estrada and his young wife "did ascetic oriental exercises, from sleeping in a sitting position to eating handfuls of raw wheat"). He was a good chess player and an amateur violinist and was particularly fond of birds; and so was his wife who, when I met her in 1966 (not quite two years after the writer's death) still walked about their house in Bahía Blanca with a tame sparrow on her head or shoulder. According to Doña Agustina her husband drove himself hard, leaving virtually no time for movies, the theater or social activity. His one indulgence was chain-smoking (the probable motivation for his short story "The Cough," about an impractical man with a legendary cough who spends more than he can afford on a costly urn for his father's ashes and whose henpecking wife finally abandons him).

His books and cultural journalism, though abundant and critically well-received, brought him little compensation, except for a very substantial National Prize for Literature in 1932. His basic income had to come from another source. For a tedious job in the morning at the Central Post Office of Buenos Aires (1916-1946) and an intellectually much more stimulating one in the afternoon as a teacher of literature at the University of La Plata's preparatory school (1924-1946) he received meager pay and a couple of modest pensions. "Holy Saturday," the longest of his twenty published stories and included here, is about the Kafkaesque existence of an overburdened employee in an absurd government office which reflects some of the author's frustrations at the post office.

"Holy Saturday," just before Easter, is supposedly Julio Nievas' last half-workday before a one-month vacation; the train for him and his family to their seaside resort leaves at 1:30 p.m. Unfortunately a change of administration is taking place (there has just been a coup d'état); thousands of folders must be refiled, and at the same time new managers and their employees are replacing their counterparts from the preceding administration. The details of the story are deliberately tedious and confusing; the office building is an ambivalent labyrinth, familiar in some aspects, new and incongruous in others. To complicate matters further, the new regime is having a raucous celebration with music and drinks, and Julio Nievas, the faithful employee of the old administration who knows most about how the office functions and misfunctions, is repeatedly called on to straighten things out. The trip originally scheduled for 1:30 is postponed until 4:00. He has to type a new report with five carbon copies before he can leave; his wife has telephoned several times while he was away from his desk. As he finally makes his way out—by then it's 3:40—the notices his young daughter, or a little girl who looks just like her, dancing on a table to the loud delight of the inaugural party. As the story ends another employee tells him he's wanted on the telephone, again. "Holy Saturday" was written in 1944, a year after the Argentine military coup of 1943 and the same year as the "palace revolt" by a group of colonels which marked the beginning of Juan Domingo Perón's rise to power.

Like the nightmarish office building in "Holy Saturday," the unfinished cathedral in "The Deluge," the gigantic hospital in "Examination Without Honor" and the country estate that has grown into a city in "Marta Riquelme" are complete, enclosed environments, extended prisons from which no escape is assumed to be possible. At least that is what the conclusions to these stories lead us to believe. In the case of "Examination Without Honor," to be sure, the heavily bandaged protagonist staggers to safety after his ordeal. But Cireneo Suárez cannot assume that his miraculous survival of an operation (the twelfth failing performance over a period of eight years by an inept intern named Gregorio Cáceres) has actually led to his freedom. In the first place he'd been the victim of a complicated conspiracy instigated by his company manager to have a fibroid that had been growing on Suárez's head for ten years removed. Every detail of his experience in the labyrinthine hospital, a secretly-managed thirty-five-building complex mostly infested by giant rats, suggests his predetermined control by hidden forces. From the day he's lured into the hospital to the second half of his operation (conducted without anaesthetics), his experience is a progressive revelation of his fate, an existential epiphany. It shows him that reality is no more than a symptom of the absurd, and as the story ends he realizes "this was not the end, but barely the beginning of something that had been plotted against him for a long time."

Different though basically analogous plots appear to underlie "The Deluge" and "Marta Riquelme." In "The Deluge" twelve-hundred inhabitants of a remote, isolated town take refuge in a large, unfinished church on a hill during a flood. The situation recalls Noah's Ark, but the theme is human survival in the contemporary world. Day after day the rains continue; food is increasingly scarce; an epidemic strikes; medicine is unavailable; two-hundred hungry dogs wait outside. A doctor, an old priest, and a young mad prophet can't attend to the people's needs. At the end there's a break in the clouds; the rain stops and for a moment a rainbow appears. But, on the last page, heavy drops begin falling once more on the anxious, uplifted faces.

In "Marta Riquelme" Martínez Estrada adapts Cervantes' device in *Don Quixote* and García Marquez's in *One Hundred*

Years of Solitude—not to forget Fernando Vidal Olmos' "Report on the Blind" section of Ernesto Sábato's novel, *On Heroes and Tombs*: four cases in which we find a work within the work attributed to a previous, imaginary author. Technically and fictitiously speaking, "Marta Riquelme" is Martínez Estrada's prologue to a 1,786-page work, Marta Riquelme's *Memoirs*. She is the most enigmatic of the author's characters and has written a testimony that mystifies more than it clarifies. William Henry Hudson had long before written a story under the same title. Hudson's Marta Riquelme, an inhabitant of the nearly tropical region of northwest Argentina, loses her husband and children and then her mind. Finally, according to her neighbors, she's transformed into a huge vulture. In a sense Martínez Estrada revives her in an urban setting. The author of the Prologue tells us that the manuscript has been lost and that he can reconstruct it only from memory and must theorize on the true personality and ultimate fate of his subject. Marta in her *Memoirs* writes both as a historian and an autobiographer. In the former role she traces the evolution of the city ("Bolívar") from the time of its foundation by her great-grandfather as a country estate ("La Magnolia"). Her grandfather converted the country home into a hotel; little by little relatives arrive from remote provinces, and houses with central patios are built around the hotel. Soon there's a need for streets and sidewalks, and the inevitable result is a seething city whose similarity to Buenos Aires is a great deal more than casual.

But the novelistic substance of the work is more significant than its essayistic motivation. Marta's family is a strange assortment of neurotics, alcoholics and suicides. Her handwriting, like her emotions, is difficult to decipher. The prologuist and editor draw conflicting inferences from the manuscript. Marta is portrayed more as a character on the threshold of development than as an intelligible protagonist. Martínez Estrada insinuates, successively, that she's innocent, angelic, passionate, treacherous, and licentious. Her love for her uncle hovers between the maternal and the erotic and is in obvious conflict with her passion for Mario, her cousin. The last sentence in the Prologue is still more perplexing than the ambiguities that precede it: "Everything that follows is simply stupendous."

Leland Chambers has given these somber tales the sensitive translation they require; through it the English-speaking reader is exposed to a turbulent soul and to the historical enigmas of a region still too far away from us.

HOLY SATURDAY

More than two weeks ago Julio Nievas applied for his annual leave of thirty working days. It was not granted because the division chiefs had been completely and unexpectedly changed just two days earlier—,on Thursday. He had it verbally approved, but by a supervisor—a very worthy man—who had been dismissed and put under arrest upon the discovery of some fraudulent delays in the office of Abstract Affairs.

The recent coup d'etat overthrew the government which by this time everyone already considered constitutional, the one which, it will be recalled, had been imposed by Captain Cruth six months earlier as a result of another revolution that in the long run had not been successful. Nothing was known yet of the fate borne by several higher officials, and the situation was much less clear for the personnel of lower rank. Julio Nievas had been a clerk for a long time, one who always fulfilled his obligations, and he had never gotten ahead. His immediate supervisor, at least until leaving the office yesterday, was an old school friend, cousin of a captain in the artillery, and he did not dare remind him of the matter. But today it was indispensable that he do so. His wife would ask him every time he came home from the office how the matter of his leave was coming. She took an interest in it as if the affair might compromise the family honor. She never for a moment thought they might relieve her husband of his post. And not because she was convinced he was just a good-natured donkey who bothered no one. Instead, she assumed that he must be pretty well situated within the new, grand scheme, and she urged him to insist to his superiors that they give him his leave, to which he had a legitimate right. Put a little energy into it so as not to let yourself be trampled on or get so chicken-hearted, and everything would be easy. There was no obstacle, naturally.

Julio and his wife Emma had a little girl, Nelly, nine years old, who studied dance and was a little fragile. The sea air would be good for her—that was the opinion of Aunt Julia, a ballet enthusiast—and Emma had a little money her aunt had given her without her husband knowing of it, to supplement their expenditures at the beach without their needing to live like miserly clerks. He was looking forward to a month's vacation at the hotel and to strolling around after bathing. They would go to the Casino too. Yesterday, Friday, he had been able to find out that his leave was granted—confirmed—and that it only lacked the signature of the Secretary for Regulatory Affairs.

"An employee such as you," he had been told, "for so long a time, one who writes poetry too, is worthy of every sort of attention. I know your background and I've seen your record book. Tomorrow, Saturday, when your work hours are done, you can simply leave, if there is no order to the contrary."

Julio ventured by way of good-natured protest, "You don't think the new Director will interpret my absence as a lack of cooperative spirit?"

The answer was categorical, and in a different, unexpected tone. "Nievas, do you think your work is so important? The Director doesn't even know you exist."

The morning of the great day, Saturday, Emma had everything ready. She and their daughter had risen early to pack the remaining clothes. Four suitcases, two of them lent by Aunt Julia, and three parcels. The little girl was in a euphoric state and went up on her toe-tips, extending her arms like a sea bird gliding in a long descent over the scene. Her father hurriedly drank his *cafe con leche.*

"Don't forget, the train leaves at one-thirty and you have to get the tickets. You arranged to say goodbye to Aunt Julia, and you still haven't gone. At least call her on the telephone, though it's not the proper way. She's loaned us her suitcases. And don't forget to notify them to shut off the phone, and turn in the change of address as soon as you finish at the Bank."

It was quite hot this morning. Julio gulped down the final swallow of his breakfast.

"I left work late yesterday and was very tired. I'll go now, before getting on the streetcar."

"Aunt Julia promised to give me something," Nelly interrupted, making her little face like a sylph's.

"I'm on my way. Goodbye now." Without pausing, Julio caught up his hat from the hook.

Still, he heard: "I hope you won't let them postpone your leave as you did your promotion. And it wouldn't be anything too much for you to make another inquiry at the Mutual Benefit Society to see if they can manage a room at the Summer Camp. It would be a fine thing if we got to the resort and didn't find a hotel."

"What do you mean, not find a hotel! All right, I'll see you later."

"Papa, you won't forget anything?"

"If you had hurried a little, you would have managed to get the fares for government officials."

He had no time to go say goodbye to the aunt because the busses passing by him were filled up, and it would have made him late. It was obligatory to sign in by the clock on entering and leaving, and only a few minutes remained to get to the office. He got there.

On the tables were dossiers stacked in compact heaps. When Julio checked through the drawers he found an unexpectedly large number of them. How had that happened?

He asked the office boy, "What are these papers?"

"The Director-in-Chief is going to visit the offices today."

"Do you mean they have taken dossiers out of the archives, or have they brought them from somewhere else in order to pretend that there is so much work?"

"I don't know, Julio."

"Has the boss come in?"

"He's been in his office since seven."

He was the first one to arrive at the office where the editing, collating, and preliminary drafts of decisions were made. The rest of his colleagues experienced the same shock upon their arrival; but none expressed surprise and everyone occupied his place and began the task without comment.

The Supervisor had put an important job under his direction. He was to take a census and make a list of all the staff by name, marital status, address, age, health, family, record book, conduct, aptitudes and complementary credits, military service, political affiliation, relatives in the military, etc.

Sixteen volumes of provisional regulations had already been published concerning the permanent, appointed, interim, replacement, would-be and current personnel, which he had to bring up to date in accord with statute, the roster, and the appendix dealing with salaries, promotions, demotions, and dismissals.

Those tasks used to be entrusted to technical personnel who would process them very slowly because of the many kinds of difficulties there were in checking the records, along with the police and civil personnel documents it was necessary to consult, often just memos that had gone from hand to hand until reaching their destination, that is, if they were not mislaid or lost before then. It had been the new administration's intention to replace all those personnel even though at the outset the new clerks might not have the practice and expertise of the former ones, so it was still preferable to stretch out the work a little longer on condition that it be done by individuals faithful to the last revolution. But owing to the recent upheavals, that order was suspended.

His desk remained in the same place, but when Nievas arrived, the office had an unfamiliar look. The previous day the piling up of furniture and papers had begun. Now the clerks were at their posts by a quarter to nine, some in shirt-sleeves, writing hastily or with the evident intention to demonstrate their good will and industriousness. Besides, there were new staff, brought in from other offices to cooperate and bring the files in arrears up-to-date. The Director-in-Chief had given the order—it was the first of innumerable ones—that in a week all these matters should be resolved, particularly the abstracts. There were hundreds, perhaps thousands of long-shelved dossiers. Until now, the clerks would attend to them parsimoniously, studying them conscientiously. Or to be exact, without giving any importance to time. Thus the files accumulated and many had been in process since the year before. The Supervisor immediately responsible—Nieva's boss—would be given short shrift if he didn't succeed in clearing them all up. Conscious of his compromising situation, his disposition changed overnight. From the friendly person he had been, he turned into a brusque one; from a tolerant to a demanding one; from courteous to rude. He began by giving them all to understand that the responsibility belonged to everyone equally, the older clerks as well as those just recently assigned to work with him. The morning, Saturday, or as it was already being called, Holy Saturday, the Section Chief would come around to give them instructions, passing through all the offices. It was possible that the Sub-Director-General and the corresponding procession would accompany him. The Section Chief understood absolutely nothing about all that gibberish in the documents, but he showed immediately that he was not in accord with the way the functionaries of the deposed government had been working. That morning he would give strict instructions and it was whispered that in the grand plan there would be transfers and dismissals reaching down to the humblest of the clerks.

Julio sat down at his desk, which he found covered with dossiers. It was impossible for him to take care of that stack in three hours, nor in three days or even three months. He would try to explain to his Supervisor that those matters were not within his jurisdiction and that the latter had inconsiderately managed to do him wrong by adding the work of others to his own. Besides, his leave had been agreed upon, word had been given, and Julio was not ready to put it off, nor would his wife consent. It was a question of how to put his case to the Supervisor. Upon seating himself, Julio discovered his penholder, and this was a sign of good luck; but nowhere did he find his inkwell, which he usually kept in his desk drawer. Maybe they had broken into it. For what reason? Were they looking during the night for some indication of guilt, any old scent that might give the new functionaries direction for initiating a suit that would keep all manner of people on their toes? They had brought in the tables and the dossiers by night, and it was indisputable, without needing a great deal of perspicacity to bring them to light, that they were a group of spies in action. Perhaps there were even some among the clerks whom they had ordered in as reinforcements from the other offices? The inkwell was not there. To get hold of another, in this state of affairs, would have required an hour. Given the facts and the circumstances, it was not opportune at this moment to announce that it was missing. There would be an investigation and, really, those who must have used force on the lock of his drawer would deny it flat out, since they no doubt had master keys to break into other cabinets, furniture, offices. He would have to look around for an inkwell, on the tables of the other clerks.

First Julio Nievas needed to get his breath a little, and he ran his hand over his head, which was perspiring copiously. It was necessary to get his bearings, to reflect, not to make any mistakes nor fall into some hastiness that would complicate affairs or make him lose time. He could not waste a minute, in reality. He looked at the heaps of files he had before him. Since he needed to speak with his Supervisor and ask permission to take care of some errands (not simple ones, though they might look it), at the same time he would bring up the impossibility of getting his work up to date. If his boss had not changed overnight, as it had seemed to Julio upon his arrival, and also according to what his colleagues had said, it was possible that he might allow him to leave even though the others were killing themselves clearing up the papers. He was friend enough of the Supervisor so as to permit himself to set forth the situation frankly. As a last resort he would tell him that it was a matter of his wife's obstinacy. And when all was said and done, it was in part his Supervisor's fault if he had not progressed in his administrative career during these past ten years, and that was the motive for his wife's judgment of him as a good-natured fellow to whom the Supervisor had denied what he granted to others. He was going to tell him everything because it was true, in part, though he wouldn't be able to do so during these critical moments while he was awaiting the visit from the Section Chief and his superior was acting like a demon! It was a truth which he would get across to him sometime, today or later, when things got calmer. Now he would only request of him, he would beg him, to allow him half an hour's time to run some errands at the Bank. With this swarm of collaborators, the dossiers would fly like the wind. Besides, it wasn't right for them to palm off dossiers on him that belonged to other clerks or other offices, as if he didn't have enough with his own. Thus he sat, pensive, the same old ideas going around in his head, in a state of confusion that debilitated and wore him out like an instant illness.

The others were working dizzily, except those old clerks who attended to advising the newcomers who in their turn, without the slightest spirit of fellowship, were augmenting the difficulties instead of putting a little good will into resolving them. When two of them were using the same narrow aisle which remained free between the desks and the piles of dossiers, they had to strain in order to squeeze by each other; other times they would decide to turn around and each one find his own path as in a labyrinth, because in order to get through it was necessary to solve the puzzle of the desks and chairs. The clerks' chairs were so close together back to back that to speak with each other, it sufficed those whose backs were together to throw themselves behindward just a little and then their cheeks were so close they could talk without anyone hearing them. In that way it was easy for them to keep up conversations and pass each other orders which the old clerks never succeeded in hearing, no matter how much they exerted themselves. In short, there was a great uneasiness, a muffled restlessness among them all. They worked intensely, but one could see by such exaggerated diligence that they were extremely irritated. Particularly the older clerks, who saw their offices invaded by contingents of incompetents bent on aggravating things as if the situation were not already bad enough. There were two parties, and the fight to the death was silently begun, each one in the tranquillity of his own task. When the Examining Magistrate would call someone to testify, that would be the moment for revealing all and for piling denunciation upon denunciation. Some would explain that the false help had merely served to hold back the work of the others, without thereby insinuating that a lack of order and foresight might previously have existed; others would expose the chaos in which the office found itself, the lack of good will among the older clerks, and some irregularities which they were marking down in the little notebooks that nearly everyone carried around and brought out stealthily in order to make furtive notations. It is also possible that the new employees were documenting some anomaly or other, some erroneous response here and there as proof of some eagerness to bring down the revolution. The new ones, as the disclosers of irregularities which until then—until their arrival—had passed unnoticed, held the best cards in the game for staying afoot and exacting justice. The old employees felt, they intuited, the conflict because the questions put to them often referred not directly to the matters they were supposed to resolve but focused on minor errors of procedure, omissions, negligent formalities, inadequate collating of the dossiers. Besides, it is possible that it may have been a question of a search which bore the assignment of seeking out mistakes instead of settling problems. That was quite possible, above all if one kept in mind that on a great many occasions the questions were either infantile or else so obvious that they demonstrated in the new clerks a profound knowledge of the technique of collecting evidence for indictments, of planning reports, and applying the rules. Of course, they were old hands too, though coming from other offices, and knew the procedures and services administration of that General Division of the Ministry as well as their antagonists, or even better. In short, they would have been able to work without so much consulting, and thus they simply caused the others to waste time, along with making them nervous.

It usually happened that when the new clerks got up to ask someone how to decide some matter, they were dispatched with little consideration. Everything was done in a mild tone and low voice, nevertheless. For the old clerks they were a hindrance; they bothered more than helped. More exactly, it was impossible to work this way, teaching clerks who were well up on their material but who feigned ignorance as if they lacked the most elemental concept of the way in which investigations ought to be handled. But it wasn't the fault of the poor clerks either, since they had been brought in from the other offices as reinforcements and suddenly found themselves in this unfortunate situation. They tried in every way to disguise their ineptitude—quite understandable—and the old clerks suspected a secret lodge had been formed, pledged to undermining their posts by attributing any little error or irregularity to them. So they had to take precautions. The old clerks were cut off from the others; that is, they didn't think the invaders should be able to put the question of competency to them nor get together for a sort of sabotage. Neither was it certain whether they had willingly engaged in sabotage or whether they had conspired to ruin the old clerks. After all, the section chiefs who remained in their posts favored them. All this came about unforeseen, without anyone's wanting it, through the pressure of the circumstances. What is certain is that each one was trying to preserve his own job. Thus, on the previous day, the first one when everybody had been crowded in together, they had already set out to be bothersome, stubborn, even insolent. When they didn't find their investigations made easier, they uttered cutting words, even disguised insults, in low voices. The worst weapon they discovered, each one on his own without having passed the word around, was to threaten the old clerks with the fact that if they could not move ahead with the new jobs and new methods of working, there would be no other remedy than to bring the report before the Administrative Examining Magistrate. Because it was inconceivable that the affairs of that office could have been paralyzed throughout more than a year while the staff remained insensible to it. Which meant that, had the recent revolution not occurred, things would have continued as before. They would not attribute all the responsibility to the Supervisor but to the staff itself, which lacked the most elemental sense of duty and sacrifice. Such were the opinions circulating secretly, which some of the old clerks were able to pick up by stretching their ears.

Julio looked at the clock on the wall: it was nine-twenty. He would not be able to do business at the Bank until ten. Neither would he be able, in fifty minutes, to settle even the simplest of the issues before him, since besides making a rough copy, each employee had to put it through the typewriter himself, with five carbon copies (it was the new system), endorse it, and put it on the desk of the Sub-Assistant Supervisor, who checked over, before the Assistant Supervisor and the Assistant Head did, the settlement drafts the Section Head was to endorse. His preoccupations were too grave for him to be distressed over the rumors that some took pleasure in divulging. He did not have enough time to begin any job, and in addition his inkwell was missing.

"Do they really want us to get all this up to date?" Julio was asked by the clerk closest to him without lifting his eyes from the dossier.

"And me, I've got to leave today for my vacation," he responded.

There were seventy-two abstract clerks in that office of no more than a hundred square meters of area. Up to four assistants were working at every desk, and the furniture was so close together it was difficult to get up and move. The dispatch tables, the typewriters, the chairs were huddled together without a chink between. They had fixed up this whole absurd arrangement the night before. Against the walls were long cupboards with glass doors where the dossiers were kept under lock and key, with the most important of them in the safe, and on upright stands were the manuals and reference books: codes, decrees, official bulletins, regulations, records, etc. Each clerk, besides, kept his dossiers in process in his desk drawer, locked, with a duplicate of each one in the possession of the Supervisor. In the corner was the Sub-Assistant Supervisor's desk and a little stand with a telephone, surrounded by and completely covered with dossiers.

Julio checked through his own dossiers and also those he found upon his desk. All were ready to attend to. None had been shelved in the archives, as he had assumed, and the entry dates were far in arrears. Possibly they had discovered them, hidden by his Supervisor, in some corner of the storeroom where the office boys made the coffee and kept the cleaning implements. This was a bad custom, an ancient one: documents kept accumulating there until the officials changed, and then they were taken out to the office and dealt with in accordance with the new orientation of the administrators. There were hardly ever enough personnel for the job. The superiors were novices who needed to be advised and brought up-to-date on the affairs and taught the routines of the office, and they would almost never succeed in getting to know what they had to do before they were replaced, being sent to other sections or thrown out into the street—and this was the more usual. The majority of the abstract clerks were new and incompetent, brought over from other offices, often with recommendations and carte blanche to do nothing at all, under the pretext of being there to acquire experience. Julio was the reference source for almost all of them, though of course some there were so proud that they preferred to spend whole days in front of cupboards filled with records, looking through books and bundles of papers. As an old and capable employee, Julio was entrusted with the most knotty and delicate matters, those in which a settlement was pronounced in disagreement with all the *whereas's*. A system with a double recoil effect, they said.

"It's impossible to handle all of this in one day," was heard from somewhere.

"Or in one week," responded another voice softly.

Someone farther away imitated the hiss of a cat whose tail has just been stepped on. The Assistant Supervisor acted as if he had not heard.

"But with the new orders, the office can't delay," exclaimed a young man with drops of hair cream falling on his neck.

The office boy entered in alarm.

"The Director-General is wandering around, with his staff. They say he's coming through here. He has been going through the offices on this floor. Watch out!"

"Warn the Assistant Supervisor."

"And why doesn't he warn *us* ?

The Assistant Supervisor heard.

"Get to work," he said without interrupting his sorting through a batch of dossiers just brought to him in a wicker basket. "The tables have to be gotten up-to-date. Boss's orders."

Julio felt his face getting warm as he thought of the great number of things he had to do that morning, apart from the work of the office. He heard his wife's tone of voice, and that of his daughter, reminding him not to forget anything. He admitted that because of his timid character he had not insisted on getting his leave approved in time, and now everything was coming down upon him at once. A moment later the office boy returned with face flushed and warned everyone by means of gestures that the Director-General and his train were approaching.

He would speak to the Supervisor, provided it would not mean his post was in peril. For the three clerks who had been fired on Thursday, the very day of the revolution, had not committed any other mistake than to stay too long in the rest room and, one of them, to leave for the day at fifteen minutes before the hour without the permission of his superior. This was not the moment to raise questions of that sort nor any other, he well understood, nor to plead the trust he had had with his boss throughout the many years they had been colleagues, until he became mired down in the same place while the other man commenced those leaps and bounds which brought him to the managership of the office, which was a jurisdictional one. Just a week earlier, even the Saturday before, those difficulties would not have implied any problems at all; everything was simple then and by now he would have been chatting and nursing his cup of coffee, waiting for ten o'clock to come so he could tell his Supervisor that he had some things to do outside the office, that he would not return, and that since his leave had been promised verbally even though the signature of the Pro-Secretary of the Division was still not on it, they could send it to him at Mar del Plata when it came back signed. Now, a week later, or more precisely, two days after the revolution, everything was completely different and there he was—a good-natured nincompoop, he felt it brutally—without the slightest idea of what in the devil to do. He rose. Instantly all his colleagues interrupted their work and watched him as if it were a question of a pose that held some danger for them. Some of the new clerks brought their hands to the pockets where they kept their little notebooks and stealthily laid them out on their desks. Julio looked at them with an expression of surprise and defiance. The several dozen clerks in the office (there used to be just twelve) were hanging on what he was going to do. In truth, it was strange that, in the midst of work, someone should have gotten up and stood there looking at them this way as if he were about to direct some words to them. Then the Sub-Assistant Supervisor, whose office was in a corner and made a little nook, and who had disappeared underneath the piles of completed dossiers which covered the chairs and nearby cabinets in addition to his desk, stretched his neck up to look. Julio went directly up to him and in few words told him he was going to see the Supervisor.

"He is busy now. Besides, you know already: a matter of minutes and the Interim Director-General will be here with his group to give direct instructions to the junior staff."

"I'll be right back. No more than a couple of words."

"Well, you know what you are doing, and I wouldn't want you to complicate my life. You are responsible for your actions. If the Interim Sub-Head, who is a retired director with fleas up his ass, I warn you, if he asks where you are, then you'll have to get the papal *nuncio* to help you out."

Amidst a general sigh and gesturing of faces and eyes, Julio returned to his place. He had not reached his desk before his name was being shouted from another corner, because someone was calling him on the telephone. Zig-zagging as best he could, turning back, going round about, he got to the apparatus. It was his wife, who for ten minutes had been wrestling with the operator, trying to get in touch with him. It seemed to her that all the services were abominably attended and that all the employees had declared shameless sabotage. And what had he been doing that he had not reported this situation to his boss? Or was it that he was afraid to talk to him, too? She reminded him in precise detail of some instructions concerning what he had to do this morning; she explained that Aunt Julia had called wishing them a good trip and that she was delighted by the school party at which Nelly had displayed her marvelous qualities as a ballerina. Above all she insisted on the half fares, for which he would have to hurry to purchase tickets. Finally, she relieved him of the necessity of buying the shoes, since she had to make a quick trip downtown anyway. In any case, if she did not call him again, they had already agreed to meet each other in the Constitution Station at 12:40, just twenty minutes before the express left for

Mar del Plata. She would go by car with the suitcases, he was not to worry about that, and could relax.

Julio listened without any eagerness to respond with more than a "Yes" or "Of course, I know."

He felt the whole weight of his destiny in those words that reached him as if from another world and were pounding him inexorably on the eardrums, on his face, and in his soul. They were the same problems as always, the same affectionate and distant tone, the same simple-mindedness in approaching desperate situations. But at the moment he felt an infinite bitterness in his whole body, as if momentarily there would be revealed to him the secret cause of his lucklessness in getting ahead and the shame of his premature aging. He even felt repugnance toward his poor little nine-year-old daughter who, as innocently as her own mother in other more serious matters, had decided with an invincible sense of vocation to dedicate herself to classical ballet. She had been attending the city-run Terpsicore Conservatory for five years, and in truth she was often a marvel as she went through dances of her own invention, so expressive, so filled with sensual purity. He felt repugnance and antipathy toward everything, the world, and the human race. Upon hanging up the receiver he wiped his nearly bald head, which was seething and spinning at once. He was returning to his place when he heard the Sub-Assistant Supervisor calling.

"If you want to see the boss, take advantage of the opportunity, for he's free now. But be back here in five minutes, because the Interim Director-General has already left his office."

Julio went off running as if impelled by the stares of everyone. He suddenly thought of an infinity of things, all the errands he had to do, not so much as actions to accomplish or as clear ideas, but as a tumult of irksome obligations thrown upon his shoulders. The Supervisor was still occupied, but his secretary told Julio the Sub-Director would be arriving soon and that the best thing was to go back to his post; that she would let him know by the office boy. The dry, brusque tone the secretary used let him know with certainty that his credit had diminished greatly in recent hours.

Julio was returning to his desk when he saw that the retired head, the Interim Director-General, was advancing down the other hallway, surrounded and followed by a great number of functionaries, many with uniforms, marching with a military and solemn bearing. The Director-General and his retinue were making their way toward his office with manifest decisiveness.

The Director-General was relatively young and wore the uniform of his grade with martial distinction. He entered surrounded by a train of some fifteen persons, all dressed in the administrative uniform; the others remained outside, and Julio Nievas mixed among them. The staff tried to get to their feet but were so jammed in that many remained crouching and others did not even move.

The orderly-herald advanced among the clerks' chairs and went to the other end of the room. Then he solemnly grasped the bugle, which he brought to his mouth, and with a strong, vibrant, and tremulous blast he blew "Attention," followed by a Reveille. The enclosure was filled with strident sounds that made the glass doors of the cupboards tremble and deafened everyone. The twenty-story building seemed to be shaking to its foundations. He played thus for half a minute. The retinue, at attention and gathered up stiffly, listened. And the clerks, some with heads bowed so low as to be resting them upon the file folders, furtively tried to stop up their ears. One might say that the whirlwind of sound was drawn toward the corner where the Sub-Assistant Supervisor was standing, for the latter was vibrating with the bugle's vibrations, goose bumps all over, with his hands pressed hard upon his ears, in a rhythmic swaying in time with the bugle. When the herald-orderly finished his prelude, the Director-General extracted from within his military blouse a piece of paper folded in four, which he had already read in similar ceremonies in the other offices. The furniture was still resonating, and the walls and the dossiers.

Snapping to attention with a sharp crack of his heels coming together, he spoke.

"All right, then. You should already be in possession of official information concerning the intentions of the new government, and that we are ready to punish all those who demonstrate bad will and stubbornness. Dismissal will be the lightest penalty, and let no one come to me with petitions and references. Let him who must, fall. All right. It is necessary to labor without watching the clock; you know the hour you enter here but not the time when you may leave. As long as there is work you have to hit it fair and square, just as I shall do, for I am the superior officer over all of you. Work dignifies, and he who works honors his country. Sit down now, and to work, boys."

The Director-General and his retinue left. He marched in the center of a row of five persons, the slimmest of them, all with uniforms and gold braid and sabers unsheathed, points toward the floor. Behind came fifty or so functionaries in parade uniforms. Running, the orderly-herald got himself in front. He seemed taller and more robust in his ordinary uniform adorned with tassels, cordons, and several colors of braid, a bicorn hat with pompoms like powder puffs, a golden shield which was the emblem of his division upon his breast, and a bugle, which he grasped, with its red, green, and blue tassels and cords, its ribbons black, white, and colored. Upon reaching the hall where the statues of eminent persons were, the formation wheeled with martial precision and stiffness, making its way in silence and enwrapped in the noise of its footsteps toward another section of the Department of Preventive Abstracts.

Julio entered. He and the rest had observed it all without blinking. These ceremonies occurred with great frequency, and the words were nearly always the same. They were published in the Bulletin by the first one who had said them, and there the secretaries found them and made the new directors learn them by heart. They formed part of the administrative ritual. While listening to them, Julio was thinking about the immense power—with regard to his own destiny as well as that of the rest of the staff—which that young fellow had in his hands. He seemed to him like a semi-god, chosen for awesome enterprises. Julio was frightened and ashamed, feeling himself impotent, under the pressure of events which had been squeezed into an indiscernible mass in his stomach. All of those in the retinue followed after the Director-General, leaving a latent threat in the the air. To each his own.

The Sub-Assistant Supervisor, without saying a word, was dividing up the dossiers, aided by the office boy. Handing a stack of them to Julio, he said to him, "Look here; I believe Campana's dossier has come back."

Julio felt a chill. It was an abstract of most pressing urgency, since a supervisor and three clerks had been suspended under the accusation of voluntary obstruction of services. Impossible to take care of that dossier in three days. He checked through the stack given him and, indeed, there was Campana's dossier.

"Here it is. Who can I transfer it to?" Nothing better occurred to him, in his frame of mind.

"Transfer it? *You* initiated it. You know the whole procedure."

"Yes, but don't forget, my leave begins today."

"Well, you know what you're doing. You heard what the new Director-General said just now. See the Supervisor about it, if you want."

"But he's not in his office right now."

"See him later, when he returns."

"Besides, they've left me all these dossiers."

"And you have to leave today, absolutely?"

"Of course! I asked for the leave two weeks ago."

"Two weeks! And you've been so calm about it! You haven't forgotten what has happened in these two weeks?"

The ring of the telephone was heard.

"Nievas. For you," announced an employee.

It was his wife, who again asked him if he had visited Aunt Julia and gotten the tickets. She had called the station and got it confirmed that the train departed at one-thirty, and that he would have to hurry to buy the tickets. She and the little girl were all ready, were even wearing smocks for the train. And he, was he going to go in his office suit?

Julio felt a great tiredness; at the same time he felt alone, forsaken, like someone who has to fight so that his enemies may triumph. It was nine-thirty. He left to talk to his Supervisor, who still had not returned. Before anything else he would have to get permission from him to leave for half an hour, to go to the Bank. First he would get his leave confirmed. On coming back to the hall, he encountered the Assistant Supervisor in the doorway. The latter said to him in a friendly tone, "Look, Nievas. Here's my opinion. The best thing for you to do is postpone your leave."

"But yesterday the Supervisor told me that the settlement was signed and only needed to be passed along."

"You'd better see the Manager of Leaves, then."

Julio left, but as he saw that his Supervisor was returning, he decided to speak to him first. He would request permission to go out, nothing more. He went into the foyer and the secretary made him sit down while she announced him. There were three people waiting.

"He says to wait a moment, Nievas." And drawing close to his ear, she said in a low voice, "He's spitting fire. Did you want to ask him for something?"

"For my leave. Besides, I wanted to go out for a few minutes."

"Take my advice, don't talk to him now."

"He himself told me yesterday that today I could go away on leave."

"Well, why don't you check back just before you go?"

"I also wanted to go out for a moment, just to the Bank. I'll go to the Leaves office, then. Meanwhile, do you want to tell him I have to go out to the Bank?"

"And where are you going to inquire?"

"To Leaves, on the seventh floor."

"No. Now it's on the third. Anyway I've already announced you, and you'll have to wait."

Several office boys went past carrying enormous stacks of dossiers. One had a big bundle of papers on his head, big packages under each arm, and other documents in his hands. He was doing it ostentatiously, to show off. He looked at Julio with a sense of propriety, as if inviting him to recognize his prowess.

"This is Roviddo. He's going to sing at the banquet this afternoon."

The buzzer sounded.

"Just a minute. It's surely for you. Wait."

The three people in the foyer remained stiff, hats dangling from one hand, between their legs, as if they had all agreed on a posture. They were staring at the floor. Through the great open windows entered a soft breeze which did not succeed in refreshing the muffled, heavy atmosphere. The great Smyrna winter carpet was still in place, a reddish purple. There was a cedar fragrance in the air from the wood panelling on the walls, the work of German cabinetmakers.

First, the secretary picked up some letters from her desk.

"I'm just going to ask him about this in passing. One moment, please. You, Mr. Arias, you know what I told you: the Supervisor can't see you today."

Arias, one of the three, no one could tell which one, remained motionless, the same as the other two.

"Arias, don't pretend you're deaf. You know you have no chance today."

"I don't care, ma'am," answered the oldest of them, who was Arias. "I'll just stay here to see if he takes pity on me later. I've got six little kids...."

The secretary disappeared with the letters. It was nine forty-five. Julio had done very little this morning, and there he was wasting time as if he were already on vacation. He recalled the Director's speech, for no reason at all. It was a collection of visual and auditory images, nothing more. He fell into a sort of stupor. "... hit it fair and square...." How could you "hit" work? That didn't seem logical. It didn't make sense. But you couldn't "*do* it fair and square" either. Other office boys were coming in with bundles and stacks of dossiers and notebooks, simulating tiredness. What a difference from Roviddo, who had to sing during the afternoon.

The head of some office came in, one he did not know.

"Taking it easy?"

"I came for my leave."

"You're going away? To Mar del Plata?"

"I hope so. If they let me."

"Lucky you. I can't get away. How are you fixed for work?"

"Smothered."

"Then they won't give you your leave. I'll be seeing you." And he extended his hand and took his leave.

When the secretary had him go in, Julio's throat was dry. He wouldn't be able to confirm the leave at all, but only get permission to go out—for a quarter of an hour, no more.

His boss was in a somber mood. He looked at him as if he didn't recognize him, without responding to his greeting. Nievas stammered out that he needed an hour's permission.

"Today! Today of all days! You are one of those who wants to sabotage me, too, friend. I know.... Well, go on, but on condition that you get your desk cleaned off today."

"Cleaned off? I've got about fifty dossiers there, and you know they let me have my leave."

"I didn't know it had been signed already."

"Signed, no. But I have it confirmed verbally by you yourself."

"Of course ... everything is very clear. You're trying to toss off the responsibility for your conduct on me, in addition to that of your work. Why do you have fifty dossiers not taken care of yet? And you come and bring me this sort of news at a time like this!"

"We've all got the same, just about. You know they brought us those dossiers that were being processed in the other offices."

"But there are more than sixty new clerks to help you."

"All together they aren't worth a single one of the old ones."

"The old ones. I am well aware.... The old ones! Here is a fact, now learn it, Nievas. As far as your leave goes, the situation today is somewhat different from when you requested it, and I imagine you must have realized that. You will have to negotiate with the Pro-Secretary to get it signed before you leave. But the office can't be left like this."

"Whatever you say. But I've already got the tickets for my wife and my daughter."

"So you're going to bring all your family problems to me, as if they mattered to me or to the Division! Or is this a new strategem of beforehand compromises, so that I'll give in? I'm tired of being condescending, Nievas. You may go."

"But do I have your permission to go out for awhile?"

"I can't prevent you, but this hour will have to be on your own time. I can't do any more for you."

"Thank you."

Julio retired. He was crushed. He thought that the best thing for him to do would be to call his wife to cancel or postpone the trip. But she wouldn't be at home now, for sure. He saw the Sub-Assistant Supervisor who was accepting dossiers carelessly and thumping at the individual pages as he examined them. He went directly up to the Sub-Assistant Supervisor and explained that he had the Supervisor's permission to absent himself for an hour, on his own time, and that it was impossible to bring all his dossiers up-to-date. His immediate superior attached no importance to his words. Julio went to the telephone and called his friend to let him know he would wait for him at the Bank, where they had to execute a loan document. It was only a matter of minutes, since everything was already prepared. Enrique, his friend, told him that now it would be necessary to first fill out some applications in the Fiscal Work Chamber, but since he would be going by there anyway he would do it. In ten minutes he would be at the Bank.

Julio went out without his hat, and before going to meet his friend he set foot toward the Telephone Union and the Post Office to suspend the phone service and put through a change-of-address. This sort of business, normally so simple, is almost impossible to get done on Saturdays. Not only were there people thronging about asking idiotic things but in addition the staff was ill-humored, annoyed, so that their responses turned out to be so vague that Julio didn't understand very well what he should do or what formalities he needed to go through. For example, filling out forms, showing his draft card and marriage certificate, his smallpox vaccination certificate, declaring the names of his wife and daughter, stating whether the forwarding of telegrams was to be at his expense, and so on. All these documents he took with him. Notwithstanding so many and such frequent obstacles opposing him at every step of the way, insuperable at the outset, in the long run he had the impression of having relieved himself of a great weight when he abandoned all those measures and went out running to the Bank.

He crossed the plaza with long steps and arrived at the Bank. The procedure he had to go through at the Bank was extremely simple: sign the loan document with his friend and pick up the money for his vacation. Of the thousand pesos, seven hundred would be for him. There was an extraordinary excitement in the streets and the plaza. It was indeed a Holy Saturday, as reports spread throughout the metropolis.

That Saturday was a day of exceptional light and temperature, as if nature were celebrating the triumph of the revolutionary arms.

The previous afternoon the advance of the troops upon Buenos Aires had been consummated, under the command of officers who, making a sacrifice of their honor and at great risk to their lives, overthrew the civil government and established a military junta. The newspapers that morning carried comments in a tone of praise but from differing points of view, remarking over the advance upon the city, the tactical movements of the troops, the officers' acts of courage.

They arrived with their mounts, they tied them to the fence protecting the Pyramid of Liberty, and burst into the House of Government, many of them without even dismounting, along with the main body of infantry and two or three mountain guns. That allegorical feat was treated as a plain historical fact, something which would signify that the armies of the interior, in their only real combat action, had thrown themselves upon the central or executive power in order to exact a change in policy from the government, which until then had been markedly in sympathy with the monarchy and Hitlerism.

"Columns ... in parallel, marching west-to-east in the direction of the river bank, with the Main Fortress and the adjacent fortified blocks of houses as their final objective, their point of encounter being marked partially by the high towers of the city which the General ... perceived through a telescope from his positions. The enemy columns' signal to advance was given to those in the plaza by means of three rockets from the area which the vanguard occupied in the New Plaza (now the Plate River Market), answered from the Fortress, which fired cannon shots of warning; commotion broke out in the streets and set all the church bells to ringing within the fortified perimeter. The sun had not yet appeared on the horizon when the first shots began to be heard in the northern part of the city. It was the left wing of the enemy column which seized control of the Retiro, a point separated from the line of defense, almost at the same time that another took control of the Catalinas. The troops following immediately to the right of those penetrated along General Lavalle and Corrientes Streets and showed their heads above the river bank at the foot of Veinticinco and Alameda Streets, consolidating themselves there by establishing communications between the Retiro, the Catalinas, and the river bank.... The route of the invasion march ...upon the heroic city of Buenos Aires in one of its greatest historic episodes remains perfectly delineated; it is desirable now to know the conclusion: ... the way in which the patriots of the

city overcame the attack and obliged its General to capitulate ...
and those who wandered lost with him through the streets
which the maps ... had wonderfully mixed up." (Mitre)

"The night was cold and dark as they almost always are....
The soldiers were citizens and each one began to tremble for
the fate of his family and home. In a moment panic took
charge over the greater part of them, and in a very short while
the ranks became disorganized and the people went in different
directions hoping to get to their homes.... A sepulchral silence
reigned in every block where it advanced; the city seemed
wrapped in a solitude so tenebrous that, according to what he
himself says, he was getting alarmed because something like
that did not seem natural to him nor was it a good omen, while
on the other hand some of his officers told him that they had
perceived muffled noises in some of the houses in front of
which they were passing as if people were hidden within, lying
in wait." (López)

From several sectors of the horizon, down from the north,
like a lobster net, armed with hooks and sticks, tumultuously at
full gallop, there was seen an interminable avalanche of
horsemen of every sort, from the landowner with his flag to the
general, the colonel, his staff, and their concubines. Gauchos
and Indians, from the Chaco, Corrientes, Patagonia and other
places in the national domain. They entered the city as if
emerging from the jails for a coup against the State. Many had
come out of cold storage plants and bore their butchers' knives
in their belts. They displayed posters glorifying shoes with
rope soles. And those hordes were soon in coordination with
the soldiers from the north. The coup had taken place many
times before but with the help of a simple change of ministers
had gone without notice. The martial figure of the guitarist
remained standing. There were no little girls to throw flowers
as they passed nor citizens to acclaim them. They entered by
night; that is, they were not observed.

"The police inspector rang the bell. It was a clerk who
answered, shabby, perspiring, with a limp and wrinkled
starched collar, loose cravat, pen stuck behind his ear, jacket of
drill and black oversleeves all dotted with ink. The Colonel-
Adjutant scribbled a note, put his seal on it, and handed the
document to the clerk: —Undertake to capture that pair with all
haste, and let the agents use every caution. Choose some with
sufficient spirit to shoot if they must....— The inspector, his
instructions to the clerk settled, took a brief look out of a
heavily barred window that looked out over the patio. Shortly a
squadron of gendarmes went out in formation, double time.
The corporal, a mestizo with a forked beard, was a veteran of a

guerrilla band years before led by Colonel Ireneo Castañón, Old Duckfoot ... Tirano Banderas strolled along, taciturn...." (Valle-Inclán)

They were the armies of the United Provinces, many with batallions made up of soldiers for economic independence, the victorious armed force of the Federals who had thrown the Unitarians into the abyss. They wanted more justice, better laws, more respect for their lives and goods. They requested the immediate closure of the congress then in session as well as the removal of present leaders. The leaders resisted and went to the fleet, the air force, the prisons, and the commisaries. They discovered all the boats and the ports come to a standstill. After tying up their horses at Liberty's feet, the soldiers scoured the city, which then was much smaller, uglier, and less populous in the sections bordering the coast. Besides, the city was going through one of its frequent epidemics of dysentery, as devastating as yellow fever and bubonic plague among some sectors of the population. The soldiers passed through the streets cheering and waving patriotic and partisan flags. They halted carriages and wrote nasty words on the streetcars and automobiles. The citizens of the city contemplated them from their balconies, some frightened, some in jubilation; they shut their wrought iron gates and their street doors out of fear that they were all going to be massacred, the women were boiling oil in gigantic cauldrons as if to deep-fry some pastry. An evening of merriment was announced for St. Bartholomew's day. The soldiers passed in front of Mitre's house and threw flowers. Afterward, in front of Yrigoyen's house and threw more flowers. The Second World War had ended only a short time ago, and their spirits were all over-excited by the defeats inflicted upon our allies, Germany, Italy, and Japan.

"Master of the city, Colonel Pagola brought together the members of the City Council along with whomever else he was able to find.... And they demanded as a consequence that the Council reassume command and proceed toward the election of a new government...." "Whether he attributed greater strength to Colonel Pagola than to the forces taking part in the night attack which this leader had managed with a daring and intrepidness worthy of a better cause, or whether he did not trust the two battalions that constituted the principal defenses of the Fort and the Plaza de la Victoria, the fact is that...." "On addressing them concerning the country, he (a name here) told them: —The campaign which up to now has been the one most discussed and least thought about, my friends, begins from this day to be the mainstay of the province, the support of the authorities.... We will bring the war to an end and seek the friendship which respects public obligations; have no confidence in those who would suggest to you any sort of subversion of order, any insubordination; repeat with me the vows we have made to support the standing of the province.—" "In consequence, Colonel Pagola brought together his forces in the Plaza de la Victoria; he placed his cannon at the mouths of the streets emptying into it; with his police he occupied all the nearby roofs that commanded the adjacent streets; and he established two strong administrative districts." (Saldías)

The armed mobs and the combined rank and file were parading as if it were a city invaded by foreigners. Little General Banderas was going back and forth with his troops, and Colonel Pagola forth and back with his. Another colonel, Del Monte, was hastening to invade with his Reds. In the morning they began to form groups and demonstrate, quietly at first, and then impassionedly. Every fifty yards or so they would give a stentorian shout and go on with a singular noise, the shuffling of their sandals. They bivouacked in the plazas, washed their feet in the fountains, dried themselves with their pennons, and fed on their roast beef. The apotheosis came during the night. They went around with torches lighting everything up like daylight. They reached the Plaza de Mayo where the horses were waiting tied up to the Pyramid. Microphones of the Blue and White Network were set up. They shouted "Hurrahs" for Bismarck, San Benito, and Pernales. The doors of the prisons and the brothels were opened, and lengthy lines of their inmates came to swell the ranks. Forty thousand agents of public order, with tear gas, Mausers, bayonets, and truncheons, defended the City Hall. Besides, the upper echelon of the Gestapo & Co. were taking part. All of them disguised as beggars, as Croats and Slovenes, with clothing in tatters, unshaven faces, armpits smeared with grease and tobacco juice. The disorder was general. Roast beef was prepared on the grass, they drank from the same fountains they had washed their feet in, and they urinated in the doctors' waiting rooms. They consumed little barrels and bottles of beer that an aboriginal Indian brewery gracefully yielded up to the hecatomb. They set out their wet pennons to dry in the sun. In the atrium of the Cathedral and in the City Hall market they deposited their offerings and vows.

"What followed then is indescribable. The hall was turned into a confused turmoil, even acts of violence. When it was noised about that the City Hall had been taken under control, police as well as riffraff began to enter the building, with their arms. An officer ..., bearing a dagger, throws himself upon the General. The latter defends himself with his native agility and fighting spirit. The council members draw close; in desperation they seize the aggressor and while some restrain him shouting, others drag the General and _____ away to the inner rooms, and carry them over the roofs to the neighboring houses. The different groups insist screaming that the General be turned over to them ... but the Dean, _____, a venerable and very respected citizen, manages to make himself heard: he praises the rights of the sacrosanct enclosure now being violated, he speaks of the glorious traditions of the City Hall, etc...." (López)

"As if they had received a password, the cavalrymen of the allied army and the scattered troops of the conquered army, together with perverts from among the city scum, launched themselves into the main streets of Buenos Aires, sacking businesses and the homes of families encountered in their abominable course."

"That was a frightful novelty for Buenos Aires. When the booty was collected in one district they went on to another, killing, violating, more and more rapacious, brutally treating their victims with filthy excessiveness that filled the devastated city with fear. Impotent in the face of that outburst of vandalism, the citizens, aided by the police, were reduced to using gunfire to defend the homes and families threatened by the iniquity and infamy being visited upon them without the slightest risk in a city humbled by its vanquishers." (Saldías)

"After having rushed into the cells, threatening the priests with death to make them give away the hiding places of those believed hidden in the convent, they penetrated into the church sword in hand and cigar in mouth.... They searched all the altars, poking their swords into every cavity ... mounted to the pulpit with drawn sword and began shouting even as a minister of the Lord was raising the consecrated species.... Some raised the skirts of the Virgin of the Immaculate Conception with the points of their sabers while others opened the blessed doors of the ciborium in the same manner.... They shattered a strongbox on the altar to Santa Rosa ... fought with their fists in the church, arguing over a bottle of wine stolen from the sacristy.... Then they went to the Pantheon and started throwing the bones of the dead around ... etc." (Ibid.)

The multitudes occupied the plazas and the adjacent streets. The city was touched by the unexpectedness of the spectacle. The *Gauleiter* spoke, and afterward General Banderas and Colonel Pagola. The crowd sang patriotic songs, *Giovinezza* and *Uber Alles*. The people raised their arms in a military salute and the generals passed beneath these arches of triumph. The field marshals went about on foot, and the priests sprinkled them with a silver aspergillium. Father Filippo

Castañeda was putting on airs before the crowd. Then followed the *candombe*, the national dance of the big formal fiestas, led by Marshal Eusebio Hereñú, who spoke in the name of the people. Afterward they set fire to the churches.

So it was only right and proper that that Saturday should have been designated "Holy Saturday."

On reaching the Bank, Julio discovered that they were doing some repairs in the entry hall. The painters had set up a large aggregate of scaffolding and some ladders which hampered the customers' passage almost completely, and the countless people crammed in there were wrestling to enter and to go out. Although the painters were performing truly dangerous acrobatic stunts, no one stopped to watch them, urged on by their own affairs. What with the revolution, there was an element of panic. The hall was packed with customers and curious folk anxious to get to the windows. They were shoving each other with their elbows and their legs. Such uncommon activity made Julio remember that the newspapers had announced the provisional government would take some important steps regarding banking policy, implying the possibility that it might seize the money on deposit with the Savings Bank and repay the depositors with securities. Perhaps this complicated apparatus of trapezes, ropes, moveable ladders, and scaffolding upon which the painters moved up and down like spiders might be a ruse to obstruct the entry of the depositors who in this case were going to withdraw their deposits. They didn't even pay attention to the fact that drops of paint might fall on them from above, much less notice the painters themselves who were doing such foolhardy stunts as swinging like monkeys. Several mothers had brought their children to witness the free performance.

At the agency windows of the Savings Bank, no fewer than five hundred people made up a triple line to withdraw their deposits. They crowded up rudely, attempting to get in ahead of those in front, using every sort of trick: they would set their elbows quietly between two persons and slip their arms ahead so as to slide their bodies through later, putting on an innocent face as if watching the painters on the ceiling. It was an artful struggle, and the triple queue was rocking with a rolling, impatient motion whose object was really not to swing back and forth so much as it was to create some advantage whenever a crack or fissure was produced in the compact mass of alarmed customers. Neither was there any lack of those who would push themselves between the legs of those in front, pretending to search for some object they had dropped in order to better their place and get closer to the windows. The orderlies and guards, scattered profusely everywhere and even as it were implanted into the masses of customers, scarcely ever succeeded in making themselves obeyed when they attempted to have them form a single line, in order. They used strident whistles and noisemakers which they shook wildly, attempting to direct this mass of bodies that seemed deprived of individual movement. The "single line" went out by one of the doors and stretched along the pavement, turning the corner until more than halfway up the next street. The nearby shops closed their steel curtains as a precaution against having their windows broken, or showcases and display stands stripped.

Besides, there were many people at the other windows. It occurred to Nievas that they could be people brought in from the interior to pretend they had business with the Bank, making access difficult for those who were really concerned and thwarting their intentions of withdrawing their money. For there were a great number of women with the look of humble circumstances about them, as well as little children crying, frightened by the tumult or the shoving. The Bank looked like the platform of a railway station where, at times of panic (this had happened during the previous revolution, six months gone), the trains whose normal departures were at fifteen minute intervals had been delayed for three hours. To advance through this silent multitude, from which the screams and crying of the children stood out like whipcracks, was an arduous task. Julio made his way resolutely to the counters of the Credit for Public Employees Section. But when he managed to get there, they told him that until a new order came these counters were set up to serve the School Savings Bank. After waiting a while and looking over the crowd, anxiously searching for his friend, he spoke to an orderly who appeared quite tranquil and who scarcely condescended to answer him. He repeated the question. Up to the second floor, next to the manager's office. The throng of people was swarming, and a sound like that of an immense beehive was buzzing underneath the great arched ceiling. Some had brought folding chairs and lunch. Many women were changing diapers on their children, pressing their heads between their legs. Customers were coming and going. Groups of students in their white smocks were bunching together in front of the School Savings counter. Fruit peddlers and a hawker of balloons and whistles, their baskets covered with woven wire, were calling out, advertising their merchandise. They were bumped into, but they preserved their equilibrium, rolling with their baskets against the customers, without losing their tempers. There was also an *empanada* vendor, whose temples 'were decorated with salves of grease and herbs. As she was rapidly selling her *empanadas*, a little ragamuffin boy was renewing her stock for her. He was using a feather duster to scare away the flies, which this morning were extremely irksome.

His friend did not appear anywhere. They had agreed to meet where he was now, right here exactly, next to the column on the left. Perhaps he had already gone upstairs, disheartened by the unexpected influx of people, and in his turn was waiting for him at the Credits Section where they had to sign the document together. Julio decided to go up. He looked for elevators or stairways, and he even began to wonder, in his confusion, if this was the Bank where they were to meet each other. He sought to convince himself by looking at the surroundings, the enormous cupola, the bannisters of the six floors, the furnishings, the moldings. These were the only things he recalled about the Bank, for the rest of it seemed to have disappeared, erased by the extraordinary number of people. The clerks, the office boys, and the guards were in an impossible humor. They didn't understand his astonishment nor that a Saturday morning might have any urgency about it, especially this Saturday, on which the whole world apparently had chosen to take care of its affairs.

Laboriously he fought his way through, and by a stairway that wound around the elevator, which was not functioning— there were some workers in the cage, with lights—he climbed to where the offices of the Manager and the members of the Board of Directors were. He inquired whether the Credit for Public Employees Section was operating there, transferred from the ground floor below. Of course; that Section was on the second floor, but one had to get up there through the door on Cangallo Street. He descended the stairs by great bounds and approached the column to the left, on the lookout for his friend. Without him he would not be able to take care of the transaction. He searched for him again in the sea of people, deciding to wait a few minutes longer.

He succeeded in getting out and began to walk briskly toward Cangallo Street to locate the Credit Office. A column four persons abreast, formed rigidly in a military manner, occupied the whole width of the sidewalk as far as the corner and, turning there, stretched more than half a block farther. It was the same line that penetrated into the broad doorway and was cut off there in front of a window like a monstrous tapeworm. Automobiles and streetcars were circulating through the streets at full speed. Pedestrians, obliged to walk on the street pavement, skillfully eluded the dangers. At the Bank door on Cangallo Street there was a cardboard sign, but it was not easy to pierce through the wall of people, hardened into a compact column.

"May I get through?" he suggested timidly.

"Go ahead."

But since nobody made room for him, he opted for going around the end of the line and sliding himself along the wall, pressed up against it, with those who were squeezing him afraid that he would insinuate himself among them. He scraped past the wall and against the bodies, and every step that he advanced was a victory. The Bank facade was broad, with a great marble staircase and a thick carpet held in place by bronze rods. On the balustrade post there was a marble statue and to one side, seated on a chair, an old man in a Bank uniform. Julio bounded up the stairs without asking anything and without the old fellow noticing his entry. On the second floor was a small waiting room and to the right there was a broad hallway with statues of Greek gods, in plaster, set into the walls and large majolica flowerpots filled with plants. At the end, a sign with a red arrow pointed to the Credit Section. There was another hallway, much narrower but just as lengthy, through which he arrived at a small office with a counter. The clerk was operating an adding machine, moving the lever after striking the keys, but instead of checks he had a book with color reproductions open by his side. Julio was attended to immediately. The formalities were finished; all that was left was the signing of the promissory note, as they had told him three days earlier, when he had presented the application. The clerk was overflowing in amiability, and his mellifluous voice imparted renewed spirit to Nievas, who found himself very depressed.

"Hasn't Señor Gutiérrez come yet?"

"Oh yes, sir; he has already signed. He was here a while ago. He arranged to return very quickly." And he answered with a smile.

"Then, can I sign it too?"

"Of course."

"Did you turn the check over to him to collect the loan?"

"No, sir. That is not possible until the promissory note is properly complete, with both signatures. Wait just one moment. You may sit down, if you wish."

When the clerk entered the room where the rest of the staff was, Julio looked around from the corner in which he found himself (at the office where the public was to be taken care of) into the long, narrow hallway. It was strange that there were no people, not even office boys, and that everything was so

modestly installed. Surely that is because they set this place up
so recently and temporarily, he thought. In the room beyond,
the typewriters and calculating machines were vibrating, along
with the light sound of voices and footsteps. Julio was
intrigued at not seeing anyone, and he recalled the throng on
the lower floor and the sidewalk pavement. It bothered him
that his friend Gutiérrez had done his part of the business
without waiting for him. Perhaps he had some other matter to
attend to. In the little office there was a desk covered with
papers, and two chairs, the tall stand with the adding machine,
a coat rack, and a small bookcase. On the extra shelf of the
adding machine stand, opened to a glowing color plate, was the
book which the clerk had been looking at while he was
pretending to run his machine. Although uneasy, Julio felt
satisfied. The clerk returned with the promissory note and a
schedule of payments, which he had him sign.

"Very good. Now, go downstairs and wait until they call
your name on the loudspeaker."

"Did Señor Gutiérrez say that he would return?"

The clerk picked up his papers and then, as if he had not
even heard the question, withdrew through the door behind the
screen, without answering.

This time he was much longer in returning.

To go down to the lower floor and wait until they called
him on the loudspeaker would be a risky venture. It meant
throwing himself defenseless into a herd of bison who would
attack him, contesting his place as if it were a matter of
protecting their young. If his friend had already finished his
business, why hadn't he waited for him? He was all right here;
at least no one was bothering him. Intrigued by the book with
the color plates which the clerk had on his stand, Julio raised
the part of the counter that closed off the entry and went behind
it into the office work space. As if he were contemplating the
maps that hung on the wall, the clear sky, the furniture, he
drew near the book. Through the stippled glass panes of the
screen he distinguished the diffuse silhouette of someone who
was spying through the slot in the door. As he approached the
book, with his head bent down, he looked toward the door on a
level with his eyebrows. The clerk entered, indifferent,
choosing to pretend that he had not been watching him.

"If you prefer to wait here," he said, back turned to him,
"please be seated."

"I wanted to know if Señor Gutiérrez had any need to
return to the office. I am very much in a hurry."

"Whatever they say at the window."

This time he looked at him head on and smiled with the same affability as before. Then Nievas looked at him carefully, and he felt as if he had known him many years before, but without managing to identify him.

"Señor Alcañaz!" Julio took it into his head to say. "Do you remember me?"

"Naturally. But you don't remember me? Yes, Alcañaz." And he smiled at him. "You remembered my name, but I'll bet you don't remember me! Twenty years or so ago we were neighbors."

Suddenly, Nievas felt that instead of having a precise memory come back to him, he was himself going back to a very humble house on the outskirts of a suburban town when Alcañaz had been a boy and he was in love with one of his five sisters.

"Now, of course! How you've changed!"

"A little; you too, though not so much. Now I'm here as an assistant."

"Are you studying architecture?"

"I graduated as a public accountant. Are you asking that because of this book?"

"It looked like you might be."

"They give us new employees a plan of the building, with views in color, to learn where the offices are located."

Nievas thought he should find out something about the family, but he held himself back and asked, "Have you been at the Bank long?"

"Two days. But I don't belong to the military infiltration, if that's what you suspected. I turned in my employment application three years ago, when I graduated, and by coincidence the very day my notice came they dismissed the whole Board of Directors *en masse*. But my appointment was already signed. Are you still with the Ministry?"

"Yes. We're having a commotion there too, because of this change in administration."

"We aren't, not here," his old and forgotten neighbor responded calmly. "Are you asking because of all those people down there on the lower floor?"

"No, because I imagine there must be a lot of Bank customers who are coming to withdraw their savings."

Alcañaz smiled and put his hand on Nievas's shoulder. "You've also had good luck that they are taking care of your business, since I have heard it said that for three months the Bank is not going to be doing any loan business."

"But ours is already agreed on, and they wouldn't annul it, I don't suppose?"

Without paying any attention to the question, Alcañaz inquired tranquilly, "Do you remember Magdalena?"

"Of course. And your mother, is she living?"

"Yes, but she is very old. Well, more aged than old. You would not recognize her either, if you saw her. And Magdalena, do you remember her?"

"Of course I do. She was a very good, very intelligent girl."

Alcañaz pressed his shoulder softly with his hand.

"She married Colonel Asmodeo. So there you are."

"I'm so glad, my friend. And I'm still just a poor old clerk."

"I know that already. At home they still remember you and get news about your life."

He withdrew his hand from Julio's shoulder and with a truly distressed look on his face he said, "I know you were not lucky in your marriage. That's life, I guess."

"Me? I can't complain. I have a little girl nine years old."

"Yes, she studies classical ballet. But you made a grave mistake when you left my sister Magdalena. You can see it now: all of us are living well, and certain that nothing bad can happen to us."

"Of course. I certainly hope so. Colonel Asmodeo too."

"But they are really going to clean house. It will be a surprise if they leave a single employee from the old regime."

"I've heard that said too. But I imagine they will take into consideration the situation of the old employees, above all those who have never gotten mixed up in political questions."

"As for you, you have been badly hurt in your career by that anonymous letter your wife sent the Minister about eight years ago. She thought she would do you a favor. But you haven't been able to get ahead since then."

"No, it wasn't that."

"Didn't they transfer you immediately when they found out she was the writer of that anonymous note? Anyway, who in the world would get the bright idea to actually denounce the Director himself, as if that could have done you any good at all!"

Nievas remained tongue-tied, as if someone had turned him inside out like a glove.

"They found that out too?" He lowered his eyes, embarrassed. "What you don't know is that that accusation was a slander."

Alcañaz struck the palm of one hand with the other.

"It's in your record. Why didn't you protest then? You would have avoided the headaches you had at that time and those you might still have coming. Especially if it's true that they are going to designate a body of inspectors to go over all the personnel records of the national, provincial, and municipal administrations."

"We'll see, when the time comes."

"Colonel Asmodeo is going to occupy a high post, as you can well imagine. He is the true author of the revolution, and any day now they will promote him to general. He won't take lower than a minister's job, I warn you."

"It's better that way. I understand that he is an upright and just man."

"More stubborn than a mule."

"Do you think I would run any danger if they named him a minister?"

"Your luck is bad; that's all I can tell you. Because of the great affection they have at home for you, Magdalena had kept some letters that led a long time ago to an awful unpleasantness. Also, I understand that you did not exactly behave yourself like a gentleman with Magdalena."

"That is correct; you should know it now, if you didn't before. Those letters and the poems that you are referring to, they probably were not my own but were copied out of some anthology. So what are you trying to say to me about this?"

"It is precisely through Colonel Asmodeo that we were always kept up-to-date about what was happening with you, and we have lamented your bad luck. You are embittered, and everything is due to the impoverishment of your character. You should not have abandoned the reins of your household; I say that to you in real sympathy."

"It seems you are trying to humiliate and threaten me, Alcañaz. I have not come here for this, really."

"I have to say these things to you, just in case you still have time to alter your destiny at all; but in truth, unless you impose your will within your own household over your wife and your daughter, since they have you frightened and subdued, I do not see how you can stay afloat."

"Well, I haven't sunk yet, my friend Alcañaz. Besides, I am determined to defend my rights and my dignity, believe me."

"I'm sure you are. But that doesn't mean anything. Those are words that occur to you so as not to admit that I am talking about your well-being. Nonetheless, you did behave rather badly with us. You knew that my mother had to endure being a widow and still give us our education, and that I was the only man of the family, though just a little kid then. And nevertheless, listen well to what I am going to say to you—"

and he drew nearer to Julio, lowering his voice to a confidential tone, as a reminder, not a reproach, "—you never took that situation into account, and you entered my house with the intention of being a seducer."

Nievas looked at him in astonishment.

"You're not in your right mind, Alcañaz," he managed to say in defense, embarrassed, crushed by those words pronounced with such complete calmness.

"In the end, it was you who were seduced, and oh, how you were! Emma Eve played with you like a cat with a ball of yarn. She pulled you apart and tangled you up again enough to make one sick. And now you have two enemies in your own home, under your very roof."

"You speak like a fool, Alcañaz. Pardon me, but I don't see where you have gotten all these crazy reports."

"And just so you can see what a noble person I am, may I do something for you? You didn't pay attention to anything. You came into my house like a conqueror, without any concern for our misery and helplessness. You were going to take advantage of a poor woman's daughters if you could, even the youngest of them, without really caring which. I remember all the details well, because they belong to that time of one's life when the facts are deeply engraved in your flesh, so that you remember them forever."

Julio had the impression that he was receiving divine punishment through the mouth of this young man whom he had scarcely recognized.

"You have nothing to get indignant about, since what I am telling you will do you good. We were living then on what we got from making matchboxes. The whole family worked; the mother and her five children, around the table, from seven in the morning until eleven at night. You would come when we were only half done with the day's work. Do you remember how Joaquina prepared the *mate*? That was an hour we lost, but at least we rested a little. You sat down by Magdalena's side in front of Mama and pretended to help us in order to permit yourself all sorts of shameful things, as much with Magdalena as with whichever girl you had on the other side of you. You touched them indecently while they continued in their work, their fingers nearly worked to the bone, working all the harder because they didn't know whether to laugh or to cry, with their legs pressed together and heads bent over. But you knew very well they couldn't get up because they were as if tied to their chairs. Mama, the same as the others, tried not to watch and to keep herself very busy, folding the bristol board for the boxes. One of us used to make the backs, another the little box where the matches went; Joaquina glued the little pieces of paper to the inside of the lid and the back of the box; Juana got the rubber bands ready (remember how they were used in those days?) with the two little wires to hold them down. I stuck the sand on the side so it would come out like sandpaper. On Saturdays my mother and Magdalena would go to the factory, about thirty blocks away, on foot, because there was no other way to get there, even though the roads might be all muddy. And they frequently were, during the winter. They carried the week's work in bags, some five thousand little boxes, and brought back the material for the entire next week. Magdalena loaded herself up with the cardboard and Mama carried a bag of sand that never weighed less than forty kilos. You saw only part of that terrible punishment. And to think that the two of them would be looking out all around for fear that you might see them loaded up like that, like two little animals! But you got up late, and visited us just in time for the *mate*! I don't need to tell you how the girls used to take turns putting on the stewpot to heat—we used to eat that at noon and at night—, fixing up the bedroom, because we all slept in one room, or going to the market, which was about fifteen blocks from the house. They had to wash the clothes, iron, sweep, and do a thousand little chores it's not worthwhile recalling. But they had to do them, and no task was insignificant. Every one was of special importance, because they all added up."

"Alcañaz," Julio interrupted, "I did know all that, and sometimes I helped you make the matchboxes. That time has gone, now; what do you gain from this cruel reproach?"

"I don't gain anything, but you do, because you certainly never understood what you were doing in the terms I am making it clear for you to see. They paid us half a centavo for each box, and at most we made seven hundred a day, everyone working sixteen hours. Total: three and a half pesos per day, from which we had to cover all our expenses. And never, it seems to me, did you find us dirty nor the house out of order, despite the fact that we lived so crowded together and in such poverty. My mother managed ... and so wisely! We bought clothes and shoes on credit, paying five pesos a fortnight; our rent cost us twenty pesos; we spent fifty to eat on. So that the balance at month's end always yielded the same amount coming in and going out. Because sometimes medicine was needed, or some oilcloth, or a seat for a cane chair, and those were additional expenses we had to be prepared for. We were condemned to sit around that table, the six of us, and we scarcely talked. When one of us got so tired we were dizzy, we got up and started to do one of the household chores, so as not to lose a minute. Mama observed everything and understood it. It was impossible for her to make things lighter for us in any way; each one of us had his share in the torture, but she carried the worst of it on her own shoulders. We were always poor, but while my father was alive, even when bad came to worse we worked things out and the older girls could go to school, without having to be ashamed of their poverty. With my father's death everything collapsed, and we were as if imprisoned beneath the rubble. Almost no one would visit us, so that your visits, which humiliated us more than consoled us, were a distraction and a torture at the same time. As the hour of your arrival drew closer, we all looked at each other and began to get uneasy, as if it were time for an injection or some bitter medicine; and on the other hand, we felt that for one or two hours we would not be so alone and abandoned. You confirmed us in the conviction that we had not been banished from the world. I was six years old and I understood it then as if it were now. I'm not inventing anything; I only recall what we all went through, twenty years ago. In addition, we were hoping for some news about the promise you made us, to get a job for Magdalena and some seamstress work for Mama, because she had once been a seamstress. But since the styles had changed, she was afraid of not being able to hold a job. And as she was so disheartened, she lost the spirit to look for sewing work. Besides, she didn't have the time to lose going from one clothing store to another. She had found this job making the matchboxes and once we began it was like a wheel that begins to spin and cannot be stopped. Confess, now, you could not have done anything for us then, with your modest office boy's job, which you disguised by changing your clothes when you came to visit us. You looked then, with your twenty-two years, as if you were the friend of deputies and division heads. And you didn't do anything to help us, either. You just benefited from our hope, from our anguish, and you tried to pick up one or two concubines gratis and have a little fun caressing and cuddling all the women in the house. You even went so far as to embrace my mother—pretending affection, or compassion, or protective tenderness—and to kiss her. I remember that scene as if I were seeing it now. We were all, as always, seated at the table, working with our aching fingers. Mama got up to turn on the hot plate and get the kettle ready for the *mate*. You went toward her, told her something I didn't hear, and put your arm around her shoulders, kissing her on the cheek. Mama pushed you away with her arm, turning around, and she told you—I'll bet you don't remember what she said then.... These are her words exactly, tell me if you remember them: —Don't just feel sorry for us, help us. How can you, when you come into this sorrowful house, how can you want to insult us and make fun of us?— You didn't answer, and you went to sit down between Juanita and Joaquina, red-faced and resentful. You did not say anything, and when you left after having your *mate*, it's true that we all thought, without saying a word to each other, that you would not return. Your game had been discovered long before, even by me and Juanita, who was not four yet. In that way you used to disguise your intentions of converting misery into ridicule very well. But the following day, when we were waiting uneasily for the time, you came with a package of crackers, greeting us as if nothing had happened. This lasted—do you know how long? One year, three months and twelve days. Colonel Asmodeo has a reliable account of your adventures as a conqueror, because Magdalena had to tell him everything before he married her: the entire conglomeration. And the Colonel really likes to document things!"

Julio went out, passing beneath the countertop that formed the entryway into the office space.

"Goodby," he said, picking up some papers he had left. "I only ask you to process my loan quickly."

"Your loan is already processed."

"And if Gutiérrez comes, tell him I'm waiting for him down on the ground floor."

"And the Colonel, or Magdalena ... don't you want to send them any message?"

"Alcañaz," Julio heaved a kind of sigh, "you are unspeakably cruel. Give me your hand, because I've known you since you were a boy and because of the affection you say they still have for me in your house. Think of me as you will, I'm not asking for pity. Everything you have said is true. It's as if I were listening to my own conscience. I have regretted it all a thousand times, being such a swine at first, and later on such a nincompoop. Only God knows what lies ahead for me."

"Take care of your daughter, that's the only thing I'm warning you about. Remember that the punishment always has some relationship to the crime."

And he held out his hand to him, smiling sweetly, like a god who has just finished sentencing a poor sinner. Nievas squeezed it vigorously, tears came to his eyes, and he set out running down the hall and down the stairs. Inadvertently he went to the left and into a storeroom for books and forms. By going on through it he was able to get out onto another street alongside the Bank. To go back would have been to lose more time. On passing through, a guard had attempted to stop him,

saying he should go out the same way he had come in. Julio
pretended he hadn't heard him and suddenly he found himself in
the street. It would have been better for him to have gone
back, as the guard had said, but now that was not possible. He
had to go all the way around the block, since four mounted
policemen blocked the way through Cangallo Street. He passed
around the end of the line and using sheer force entered the
main lobby on the ground floor. Finally he distinguished his
friend Gutiérrez. He felt debilitated, he was moving along as if
being carried involuntarily by his legs, the same as if he were
getting up after falling off a horse and being dragged along the
ground. His friend was in line, behind a woman in a very short
skirt, hair artificially blond, her eyes and mouth brazenly
painted. He approached, observing his friend who was talking
to the woman over her shoulder, with his face glued to her ear.
It seemed to him that Gutiérrez was kissing her furtively on the
cheeck and neck. She was laughing nervously, with a
convulsive laughter that was shaking her all over. He got in
front of them so his friend would see him, but Gutiérrez was
very involved in his conversation, pushed into it by those
behind and intentionally pressing himself against that
scandalous woman.

Julio sought to make sure that it was Gutiérrez. But his
friend gazed at him with indifference. He wondered if it was a
question of someone quite like him, identical, and feared to
address him. Anything could happen, in his state of mind, after
what had occurred in the Credit Section.

"Gutiérrez," he dared to mumble.

It really was Gutiérrez, because he responded with a wink
and made a sign for him to keep quiet.

"I've been looking for you for an hour. What are you
doing here?"

With his hand, Gutiérrez beckoned him to approach.

Then the woman turned and said something into the ear of
her boyfriend, who inclined his head until he was brushing the
back of her neck with his chin. And they kept up a secret
dialogue that way. It seemed to Nievas that they were mocking
him. When he got close to Gutiérrez, the latter said, "You
must be getting annoyed."

"Did they already call?"

"For me, yes. I've just come from there."

"That's good. I was here earlier."

While he was speaking, Gutiérrez passed his arm around
the waist of the young woman. She put into his hand a little
piece of paper that she had taken from her purse and, turning
toward him again, she spoke into his ear.

"Didn't you hear whether they called me on the loudspeaker?" Julio asked in a determined tone. "Don't forget that I am really in a hurry, it's making me late, and I have a stack of dossiers to attend to."

At the window, quite amused, the clerk who was taking care of it was conversing with one of the customers without being concerned about the great number of people still waiting. The one standing at his side was filing his fingernails carefully.

"I don't know," Gutiérrez answered without moving. "You are the one who is most concerned about all this. Why didn't you check, if you have been walking around here for an hour?"

"We have to go together."

"Go where?"

"To withdraw the money. They told me upstairs that I would be called on the loudspeaker."

"All you need to know is, which clerk? There are about twenty, and each one screeching louder than any of the others. It's not bad right here, believe me. Right, sweetheart?"

The woman started to laugh, as if those words were funny to her, and she began to shift her position with the intention of shoving Gutiérrez out of the line. When he had left, bumping into other, no less suffocating clumps of customers, Nievas asked him, "Who is she?"

"It says on this little piece of paper," Gutiérrez answered, putting it in his pocket. "It's a plot. Or didn't you pay attention?"

"Yes, but the fact is we have other more important things to do."

"Important for you, because you're getting two thirds of the loan."

"Come on," Nievas responded, making his way courageously.

"I haven't budged from here on purpose, just waiting for you, and still you're getting fidgety. Do you think I don't have anything else to do today?"

They tried to get close to a window. Those who were waiting pointed out to them, ill-temperedly, that they should place themselves at the end of the line. They asked a guard who was wandering around there, and he suggested that it was possibly in another lobby. At least they used to pay the money out in the other lobby, though no one now knew where it was. They started toward it when they heard on a loudspeaker, "Gutiérrez and party. Go to the Credit Section for federal employees, Cangallo Street entrance, second floor."

"Good. They're calling us now."

"We have to go upstairs again."

"What's supposed to happen?"

"Our transaction was already completed; that's what the idiot who takes care of things upstairs told me."

"Idiot? He's a real bastard, with his cheap tricks!"

After a great deal of effort, having to go around the whole block, the two of them arrived at the little office on the second floor. The clerk attended to them with the extreme courtesy which was his nature, and giving them a friendly smile, told them there was nothing for them to do there, that the affair was taken care of, and they only needed to wait to be called on the loudspeaker in the ground floor lobby. It was possible that it had something to do with some other transaction. And the clerk went back again into the room where the typewriter keys and the whirring of the calculating machines sounded amid the rustling of voices and of footsteps. They were alone.

"Why did you call him 'the idiot who takes care of things upstairs?' He's very courteous. Talking with him is a pleasure."

"Are you going to wait here just to talk with him? I'm leaving. I can't do any more; my nerves.... Look, Gutiérrez, my friend, I ask you, for God's sake!"

They returned to the lobby. The blond woman had disappeared. Gutiérrez searched for her with real anxiety. He was moving his head about, lifting it up with his eyes wide open as if having a hallucination. Nievas pulled him by the sleeve, making way for him through the crowd. At the end of a few minutes as long as hours, they heard a loudspeaker from over their shoulders: "Gutiérrez and Nievas: credit number zero two two nine three five eight fourteen B. Repeat: attention, Gutiérrez and Nievas, credit number zero, two, two, nine, three, five, eight, fourteen B. Window six, to cash a check."

Finally they reached the window, where there were few people. They turned over the check for a thousand pesos, after signing it, and without major setbacks, at another window (this one with lots of people); the thousand pesos they were given in exchange for the check was in radiant bills of fifty and a hundred. Once it was divided, which in the end amounted to seven hundred pesos for Julio and three hundred for Gutiérrez, the former asked his friend while he was putting his money in his billfold, "Now are going to look for the blonde? Well, good luck. And see you later."

Without hearing what his friend answered, he went out as soon as he could, forcing his way through the crowds. He bought the train tickets and set out toward the office. He was beginning to feel relieved. The clerk Alcañaz's warnings and reproaches were the only thing weighing on his soul. But everything had taken place in such a whirlwind, and it seemed to him that he himself had spoken so harshly as to add to his tribulations.

As he entered the office, the Assistant Supervisor looked at his watch and, without turning toward him, said "Someone called you twice from your house."

Julio looked aorund him, at the clerks and the tables crowded with dossiers. There was a great difference in all of it, after his return. Before, it had been a tumult, a motley, a heap of hostile bodies, and himself a contemptible being, overwhelmed by obligations and menacing affairs, completely crushed; now it was they who seemed forced into distressing work, and himself a free man, with his tickets in his pocket and the formalities at the Bank all arranged. But before him, in their stacks of pink portfolios, there were the fifty dossiers which reminded him of the Supervisor's order. An order that no doubt was elastic and revocable, but one which in the present circumstances might be the origin of some serious trouble. First he wanted to talk to the Sub-Assistant Supervisor. His inkwell was missing, and he was certain that he had left it in his desk drawer, as always. Absolutely certain, although he had neither proof nor witness, nor was that even the place to leave an inkwell. Still and all, if the Supervisor were to come passing through, and he might do so despite his kindly nature simply because of the influence of the atmosphere and the tension of recent days, he could not insist that his inkwell had been stolen from him. He would have to find the right way to present his complaint without its being interpreted as a denunciation. Because that would give rise to an investigation, and things would get much more complicated than they already were. Of course not; because for that he had to be certain the new clerks had broken into his drawer—something of which he had neither documentary proof nor testimony. It was necessary to proceed with caution. Maybe to ask for another inkwell, without alluding to theft or secuestration or confiscation. Right where he was standing now, it was difficult to retreat or to advance. He was exactly the same distance from his own table as he was from the Sub-Assistant Supervisor's. He opted for retreating and talking to him about his dossiers. He did so. The Sub-Assistant Supervisor was overwhelmed with work and in a state of physiological torpor. His lower jaw hung down in stupefied lassitude, his eyes opaque and his complexion like parchment. Nievas had not noticed whether he had looked like this when he came in, but it was almost impossible, more precisely, absolutely impossible, that such organic decay could have been produced in the course of half an hour. When he asked about his leave and whether he could transfer his dossiers to others, the Sub-Assistant Supervisor turned a languid, imploring gaze upon him and answered with brutal incomprehension, "Here everyone saves his own skin. Don't come to me just to throw garbage at me."

"But, what does Esteban say? I talk to him about administrative things. He knows my leave is pending and that I am covered with work."

"I'm covered, too; smothered; buried—" and he drew confidentially close to Nievas. "Don't look now, but all those dossiers I have on top of the cupboards along this wall have been done fraudulently: topsy turvy! It's the new clerks; just sabotage. The boss is already busy with the reports and this afternoon, when everyone has gone, those dossiers are finally going to get to the Court of Administrative Instruction. I'm telling you so you can see if there are any of yours in there, and save yourself some time."

"Mine, no; I know there's none of mine there. I have always worked faithfully according to my knowledge and understanding."

"But everyone doesn't work that way."

And he let his jaw drop further while he seemed to be waiting for the return of a fierce pain in his tooth.

"The best thing for you to do is to postpone your leave and come in this afternoon and tomorrow, to work and gain the time. I'm coming in, too."

"That's impossible," replied Julio in such a loud voice that many raised their heads to look at him. Some were taking out their little notebooks and waiting to hear their conversation. There was none. Instantly, Julio arose in order to make his way to the Supervisor's office. There were many people waiting. One of them was a clerk under indictment who for six months had been making the rounds without anyone's agreeing to see him. He was a scamp. When the secretary saw Julio come in, she got up and took him to one side, saying, "I was waiting for you. I didn't know if you had returned from your business. The Supervisor has asked me to tell you your leave is bogged down. The Pro-Secretary-General has not come in this morning and possibly won't even come for the party. Today is the confirmation party for the new Director-General. Terrific!"

"Did you say anything about my dossiers?"

"No. He has a thousand things on his mind. This afternoon all the higher superiors are coming with their families. It is advisable for you to see him right away because he probably is going to leave."

"May I go in now?"

"He is busy. But they'll come out right away. They are a couple of tattletales, the kind that go at each other tooth and nail. Just call them stoolies! Tell me, did you see who is here?"

"Yes. By now my draft of the petition for recovery must have been signed. A swine."

"Don't you believe it. The very informers with the boss right now have references for this guy with them, and they have muddled things up so as to make one afraid in the Court of Administrative Instruction."

"They're done for. The investigation is conclusive. Definite proof. I myself took care of it."

"You? It's a fine mess you've gotten mixed up in!"

"I haven't gotten myself mixed up in any mess. And what do they want now?"

"They're requesting the annulment of everything done so far, and at the same time they're accusing the Department of Traffic and Combustibles."

"The whole department?"

"Just the higher-ups. Two of them are already suspended. It's a serious matter."

"All right then, I have things to do. If those people are going to take so long, it's better for me to go and get my own things done."

"This guy is coming now to present evidence."

"Let him do it."

"He wants to make a claim. You're going to have to take the sworn declaration. I heard the Supervisor talking about a deposition. And it was you who got the brief together. Everyone here is going to sign as a witness."

"And isn't there anyone else to take the deposition? Why me, when I have just gotten the tickets to leave on the one o'clock train?"

"Talk to the Supervisor, then."

"Let me go in."

"He's busy now."

And the secretary withdrew behind her desk, leaving him alone. He looked at the sullen man who was sitting there with the air of a poor wretch, with his legs spread apart, hat dangling in his hands. He had a notion to address him to ask if he was really persisting in his suit. But suddenly he decided to return to his office. They would call him.

He saw that there were many clerks standing close to his desk, surrounding it. Seated upon the desk top with his feet resting on a chair was a little man, doubtless a dwarf, dressed in knickers, a little corduroy jacket, and a silk kerchief at his neck. The clerks appeared to be having fun questioning him, and he, as high-spirited as they were, kept up the chatting with a joyful face. Julio stopped short.

"Your Uncle Jerónimo, how about about that?" said a clerk.

"What does he want?"

The stranger directed his blue, inexpressive eyes toward him.

"Don't you know me? I'm your Uncle Jerónimo."

He held out his hand toward him at the same time he stretched up to kiss him, getting to his feet on the chair. This caused unusual excitement among the other clerks, who whispered among themselves, leaning backward in their seats so they could speak in low voices.

"And how is it you have come here, Uncle, and especially today?"

"What else do you want?" he sat down again. "I considered going to your house, but I thought your wife would not be pleased. I go around so poorly dressed."

"But still, you show up here, in the office."

"I understood you were going to be irritated, Julio. I couldn't do anything else. I'm very sick."

And he remained pensive, as if that illness were the source of a profound meditation which he might have to initiate all over again each time he spoke about it.

The Sub-Assistant Supervisor raised his head frequently with his sleepwalker's air, to direct an inquiring glance at Nievas. The latter was looking at his uncle, who was very old, looking extremely aged since the last time he had seen him, twenty years previously. Here in this very place. His uncle had been relatively young then, well-dressed, and it was a cause of pride for him to have his uncle looking for him at the office. He had not seemed like a dwarf then. Age had made him smaller, wearing out his body like his clothing. He used to own land, country properties, and the look of a rancher had been perceptible the moment he entered. He used to stay in the best hotels on the Avenida de Mayo, he always drove in a car, and he paid every time they went out together. Now here he was, seated on the desk facing his chair, like a wretched doll, in his working place among the papers, with his threadbare corduroy coat, his cuffs ravelling out, buttons broken, hair white, face covered with wrinkles. That hat placed atop a pile of dossiers, with its discolored and grimy hatband, belonged to him, to his uncle. The little man was silent, as if he had committed an unpardonable offense. He dropped his head.

"What's wrong with you, then?"

When his uncle raised his face Julio saw that he had been weeping and that his cheeks were damp and shining. His only reply was to snuffle forcefully. He drew out an enormous handkerchief, wrinkled and filthy, to wipe his eyes and face. Afterwards he blew his nose. Everyone contemplated that strange sight without being able to hold back their laughter, and Julio was without a doubt the most astonished about what was taking place. He looked at his colleagues who nodded their heads, contemplating him askance. Some were laughing aloud, unable to hold out any longer. He looked at the Sub-Assistant Supervisor and saw that he too was laughing, alone, as if he had suddenly recovered his former energies.

"I can't take care of you here."

"I understand; this is not the right place. But I didn't dare come to your house. Besides, I don't know where you live. I've heard you have a very cute little girl who studies dance."

"And what are you ill from?"

He looked at him with shame, irritation, pain. Was it possible that his Uncle Jerónimo was reduced to this state, that he had descended to this extreme?

"Mr. Nievas, telephone!" shouted someone from the corner in the back. Julio leapt up as if that opportunity to talk on the telephone would permit him to get away from his uncle, and perhaps if he went away the old man would disappear or might turn out to be some other clerk's uncle. Immediately after Julio withdrew they began to question the old man from all sides, as in a judicial interrogation. Uncle Jerónimo was perplexed, above all in the face of questions that were without doubt indiscreet and quite insolent. For example, whether he was a dwarf all over equally in all his parts; whether had left his broom at the door when he came in; if he was Nievas's uncle on his father's side or the mother's; whether he had his clothes made to order, etc. He responded with wit and good faith, as if it were necessary to go through this disgraceful show in order to be helped, just as those who are sick answer the most shameless questions put to them by the nurses. Meanwhile Julio was talking with his wife, who told him she had bought those little shoes, they were so cute, she asked him if he had gotten the errands done yet and advised him not to forget to say goodby to Aunt Julia. She reminded him that Aunt Julia had provided them with some of the money for their vacation, which he was to return in monthly installments. It wasn't right that he should forget to pay his respects. Julio told her that they couldn't take the train at one o'clock. He said he had too much work, and other "headaches"; that they would have a quiet lunch. They would take the four o'clock train. They should wait in the waiting room until he arrived. There was no other way. It was not a question of the Supervisor walking all over him, nor of his not knowing how to make himself valued. It was a question of one investigation, and no more. He listened to all her reprimands, and with an infinite sense of desolation he returned to his place. There was his Uncle Jerónimo in animated conversation with the numerous clerks surrounding him. Upon seeing that Julio had come back, they all returned to their desks and went back to their work.

"So you really are sick?"

"I was staying in a boarding house, on Constitution Street, until I could manage to get myself into a home. I've been here ten days. Yesterday someone stole my wallet and now I don't even have enough to pay for my meals. It had a few pesos in it, the last I had left."

"Do you need money, then?"

"More than anything I need to get into a home. I am very ill. I went around to all the hospitals. But if you don't have at least one doctor, it's impossible to get in."

"I don't know any. And what do you have?"

"Cancer."

He threw his head back and opened his mouth. On the edge of his tongue was a violet, pimpled sore. Julio was moved.

"And me, what can I do, Uncle? This afternoon I have to leave on the train, and I won't be back for a month."

"If you could get me a recommendation...."

"I can give you a few pesos, not much. I've so many expenses. Let's see what we can arrange."

"I thought you would know people in the hospitals ... since you have such a good job here."

This supposition sent a chill through Julio. He had not had a promotion for ten years. Many of his less deserving colleagues had been advanced over him. He heard sarcasm on the lips of the doomed man. All the shame that he was suffering with such great effort was concentrated through that punctilious proof of his destiny. He understood that everything was intertwined through reasons unknown to him, and his wife's pronouncement that he had not gotten ahead because of his lack of character presented itself to him as a judgment without appeal. He drew his wallet from his pocket and offered fifty pesos to his uncle. The latter stood still, looking at him.

"You can't look for a recommendation for me, then?"

"Take it," he said in a loud voice, as if for everyone around to hear him. "It's all I can do for you."

"Any hospital at all. The thing is, not to die like a dog in the street."

He took the fifty pesos and held them between the tips of his fingers. Julio led him among the desks, opening a path for him. The uncle came along behind, in tow. He waved as he went past each row of desks, as if they were all his acquaintances. To those whom he had been conversing with earlier he extended his hand. They went out. Julio took advantage of the opportunity to go to the Supervisor's office. The latter had gone. He left clear instructions. The leave was on his desk, signed. But Julio was to be informed in writing about an order. It stipulated that he could not begin his leave until he had properly straightened out the file on the investigation of the fuel theft. He felt hot and cold at the same time. That was a three-day job. The secretary handed him a new deposition by the accused, eight pages long. It was an allegation which invalidated everything that had been taken down before. He accused the higher-ups in Traffic and alleged intentional delays, implicating the Sub-Assistant Supervisor.

"You have to add this to the file and request the records that have been put into the archives," she said. "That ought to have been done before. The file on his dismissal. Here we only have the new presentation and the subsequent statements.

"The boss wants you to make a file with all the actions taken and work up a definitive settlement. Now there are some other people in charge of things ..." and whispering to him, "...that little creep is really hand in glove with the Director-General."

"And what is there to settle? Does it cancel out everything done before? The best thing would be to send the actions taken to the Court of Administrative Instruction."

"The Court already has work enough for three years. Now they have requested all the records of suspensions and dismissals for the past five years."

"Bigini's must be among them. How am I going to manage, then?"

"They begin in the year 1932. When did they dismiss Bigini?"

"Six months ago."

"Then, do you think they've asked for that dossier? Besides, I can't tell you anything more than the boss told me to."

"I'll go see the Assistant Supervisor."

"The Assistant Supervisor left with the boss."

"The Sub-Assistant Supervisor, then." He looked at his watch. It was twelve-fifteen. "Look what time it is."

"So what did you do all morning? Wandering around, receiving visitors, talking on the telephone."

He put Bigini's newest statement under his arm and returned to his office with it. On entering, the Sub-Assistant Supervisor called to him.

"Was that a relative of yours, that man who was sitting on your desk?"

"Yes."

"He came in without asking permission. Besides, visitors are prohibited."

"I know that already. He is a sick relative who's very poor."

"You could see that a mile away. But you allowed him to sit on your desk. It looked as though you were the visitor."

"Is that why you called me? I thought you were going to talk about this matter—" and he showed him the pages of the petition. "This could be more interesting to you."

"I know about it. The boss told me that you should be notified that until file 33565 is taken care of, you can't get your leave."

"I have enough here for all day and all night."

"You are supposed to know about this. You are hereby notified." And he showed him the memo.

"Remember, you're notifying me at twelve-twenty."

"To hell with the time; that has nothing to do with the order. You still have to do it, even if it's twelve midnight. I think you know that well enough."

"Yes. But remember that it's the day I have to leave on my trip."

"And what have you been doing all morning? Strolling around, chatting receiving visitors, talking on the telephone. You haven't written a single letter."

"That's because someone stole my inkwell."

"And you're just now reporting it?"

"And the other dossiers, who do I leave them with? Or do I have to take care of them too?"

"No, the others, no. It will be enough if you do 33565. Make out a list of them and turn them over to me. I'll give you a receipt. Put down the number of each file and the number of pages. With a carbon copy, of course."

"There are about fifty. I used to have six, and yesterday they dropped the others on me. If you think that is right...."

"If you don't think it's right, then put your complaint down in writing."

He was called to the telephone. It was his wife. Three times she had called, and they kept telling her he was busy with the ambassador from Bulgaria. That was the limit! She was asking him now if they definitely would not be taking the one o'clock train, and if he had talked to Aunt Julia. She thought the business about the ambassador was just a bad joke, and that even the telephone operator was mocking them now, the family included. And as far as the aunt was concerned, that was just negligence. That was how she explained his not being given the leave in time, that they had been deceiving him like a little child because he didn't know how to stand up for his rights....

The clerks had disappeared and the room was empty, though with a portion of the mountains of dossiers still on the desks.

Julio whispered to the Sub-Assistant Supervisor, "I need some records, and now there's probably no one in the archives room."

"Find out. Why didn't you request those records before? It seems to me that's just elemental."

"I already told you, I had things to attend to this morning."

"But not office things. Anyway, you've been without your inkwell up until now."

He opened a drawer and extracted an inkwell.

"Here it is."

"So *you* had it? Why did you keep it?"

"You left it on top of your desk, under a stack of dossiers. I wanted to see what kind of eagerness you had for working. But apparently it's all the same to you whether you have your tools or not, whether you're working or not. Here it is."

"In that case I don't know either if it really is the boss's order that I have to take care of this damned dossier before I leave. Remember that I've got Bigini's here, too, to top it all off."

"You ought to know if it's damned or not. I haven't seen it for two months."

He went on going through his file.

Julio left the inkwell and the file on top of his desk and went out to look for the records in Archives. There wouldn't be anyone there, he was certain. As he went past the Supervisor's office he encountered the secretary. Berdier was in his chair. She called to him from the door. "Did you go to see the boss?"

"Yes."

"Did you finish the dossier yet? Mr. Berdier is waiting here."

"Waiting? He may as well have lunch and take a nap. I don't have the other records yet."

"Oh, take your time, I'm in no hurry," Berdier broke in, as if he had discovered some little dodge of the clerk's. "Since it has to go to be signed today, I'll just wait so I can tell the Head if it's been settled as they promised or not."

"Is anyone in Archives? I also have Bigini's business. I'll do both while I'm there."

"The guard at least should be there. But they aren't going to turn any records over to you without a written order. You know that, I suppose."

"I only want to have a quick look."

He went on toward Archives, in a hurry. Berdier followed him. He reached the elevator. Berdier said in a friendly tone, "I'll go with you."

"To Archives?"

"Sure; Archives, or wherever you're going."

"I'm going to Archives to get the file on your dismissal."

"If Archives is where you're going, I'll go with you."

In the elevator they rose to the top floor, the twentieth. The immense building belonging to the Department was empty. They only saw the soldiers who had been occupying the building for the past few days, walking back and forth with Mausers in their arms, cradled like infants. While the elevator was going up they said nothing to each other. Julio set off resolutely down the hall, from which many doors led, all of them shut. Berdier hurried to keep up with him. At the end of that long passageway they turned, and the light, which came in through large, ample mansard windows, illuminated all of the hallway where the offices of Archives were located, taking up nearly the whole floor. The two first doors were closed.

"There doesn't appear to be anyone here," said Berdier.

"Let's see."

The next door was open. It led to an immense room full of shelves so close to each other that hardly any room was left between them. On those shelves were the boxes in which the dossiers were kept. When they had passed half a dozen of those narrow alleyways of cardboard boxes, Berdier disappeared. He was going down other aisles as if trying to gain time and arrive first. It was necessary for them to get to the back of the room, where the office of the Head was; Berdier knew those torturous paths well, since he had been there many times during the process of his investigation, managing to become friends with the clerks and their Head. The latter was not in the office; but the person in charge of the guards was in the office of the Assistant Head. In another room were some clerks wielding huge books. When Julio came up, Berdier was talking to the Assistant Head. He didn't need to explain the motive for his arrival, since the latter was already opening the safe and extracting from it the dossier by which Berdier had been relieved of his office two months previous.

"*Everything was anticipated,*" Julio thought. "*Now I see why there was so much haste.*"

"I came for file number 16328 MT. To look at it."

"Here it is. Are you thinking of taking it with you?" asked the Assistant Head.

"If you would lend it to me for just one moment, I would prefer that."

"Do you have an order?"

"No, because the Supervisor has left."

"Lend it to him," said Berdier. "He only needs to take down a few pieces of information."

While Julio was noting down some page numbers and transcribing some paragraphs, Berdier was in a corner of the office talking with the Assistant Head, who was quite attentive. Soon he called to Julio and beckoned for him to come over.

"I don't know if you have any special instructions for settling the matter. But I ought to give you some suggestions, to save you time. González, the Head, not only is interested in having me back, declaring the previous investigation to have been defective, but also in getting it expressly on record that they had gone ahead precipitately and without the proofs indispensable for adopting a measure of such seriousness as the one promulgated against me. Is that not true, Mr. Pita?"

"I don't have exact instructions," Julio declared. "I have only received orders to take care of this dossier today, before leaving. That's why I am here."

"Well, good. We must talk to each other with complete frankness."

"I think that is best," affirmed the Assistant Head.

"Come on."

And Berdier led them through that labyrinth with the consummate ease of a harbor pilot to a point among the five thousand dossiers of the letter D, where the most absolute murkiness reigned.

"If you will permit me," Julio was saying as they moved ahead more and more deeply into the depths of that night constructed like a grid, "The fact is that I need to save time.... I don't have a minute to lose, since I have to write up the decision with five carbons."

This slipped out because of his need to let them know what his distressing situation was like. They reached the place.

"You will save time," Berdier replied. "Let's get down to brass tacks. Mr. Migues, the Supervisor, is aware of all this. For ten years, now, I have been a secret agent of the administrative police. So the investigation, the depositions, and the slander you have raised against me have been a fiction."

"I, at least, have not committed any slander," Julio corrected him in the shadows. He saw the silhouette of his companions only vaguely, against an even darker background, cut out of a depth even more obscure.

"The time has arrived for clarifying all these old problems. In the first place, Mr. Pita, what is your opinion of the accusation with which you are already acquainted?"

"I judge that Mr. Nievas himself should explain it. And here he is, of course."

"Good; the suspicion is, Mr. Nievas, that a detective came to visit you today disguised as a beggar."

The Assistant Head interrupted, "Add that this happened after you went out for unexplained reasons on two occasions, during one of which you visited the Post Office, the Telephone Union, and the National Bank."

"Of course I went out. Errands related to my trip to Mar del Plata."

"We will talk about that shortly. Explain your visitor, then."

"He's not a beggar as you are saying, perhaps just to embarrass me. He is an uncle I have not seen in more than twenty years. He just came in looking like that, and he is very ill. Besides, someone stole his wallet with the little money he had left to take care of his illness."

"Yes, that is at least the explanation which is circulating and which everyone knows."

"There is nothing else; it is the truth."

"You gave him money."

"Yes, I gave him fifty pesos, which he left beneath the blotting pad. I have them here."

"It is part of a considerable sum you received today."

"It was not a 'considerable sum.' It was seven hundred pesos from a loan I took out at the National Bank with Gutiérrez. But why is it I who am being questioned like a criminal?"

"Oh, it's nothing like that, Mr. Nievas. I'm surprised that you have so little common sense as to think this is all a matter of a joke. Or are you unaware of the situation in which the country finds itself? Not only are all the public administration personnel on call, but the employees of this Department find themselves detained for questioning."

"I never even suspected it. Tell me what to do then."

While he was being interrogated and was responding, Julio had the impression that nothing of what was happening was real. Rather as if he had suffered a loss of consciousness, and now, in hell, his martyrdom were beginning with proceedings that were gradually getting worse and worse and that would doubtless reach the level of the infinite and the unimaginable. So that when he had said, "Tell me what to do, then," what he had wanted to say was, "Let's continue; now I understand the whole mystery."

"So you still insist that it really was a question of an uncle whom you did not recognize at first and whom you helped with a little bit of money, fifty pesos, from the sum you had withdrawn from the bank. All right, then. Remember that, Mr. Pita. There were also some telephone calls."

"Yes, of course; my wife. We were supposed to have taken the train at one."

"Do you know your Supervisor has been arrested and detained incommunicado?"

"No. I thought he had left early to get ready for the party this afternoon."

"All that is true. He did leave with that intention. But are you really unaware that he is under arrest, incommunicado?"

"No. Word of honor, I was unaware of it. And it takes me completely by surprise because I don't understand what offense he could have committed if, as you say, all this is related to the indictment that was brought against you two months ago. I can assure you that those proceedings were correctly carried out, since I myself have been involved with them after the investigation was concluded."

"Investigation, you call it. So you have no idea what that indictment signified?"

"No, I really don't. Not the slightest."

The Assistant Head went on as if he were continuing the conversation and it had been he who had been speaking previously. "But, Mr. Nievas, didn't you try yesterday to have File Number 16328 MT disappear? That's why I was keeping it in my safe."

"An unnecessary precaution, of course," Julio succeeded in saying. "I never attempted any such removal. I only sent an office boy to find out the date it had been shelved in Archives so that the Supervisor could request it in writing."

"But the office boy did not understand it that way; he understood it as something completely different."

"All right. You can go back to your work. Continue taking notes; I don't want to delay you any longer. Nonetheless, I believe this little dialogue will be useful to you so you won't waste time in reconstructing and refuting the earlier arguments. You possess the key. Now it should only take you a few words to cancel the charges against me which, you will notice as you check through the proceedings using this key, are simply false."

"Let me ask you first if this staff situation means that something might get in the way of my leaving for Mar del Plata today."

"None at all, since you continue to belong to the MInistry. I don't believe you have anything to fear. My opinion is that you had no complicity with any of the higher-ups."

"That's true. I am grateful to you."

They left. Julio continued to leaf through the file, but everything seemed muddled, as if he had lost one whole hemisphere of his brain. He ran his hand over his head. He looked around and saw that Berdier, the Assistant Head, and the other employees of Archives were together in the registry office, talking in low voices. He couldn't imagine what was happening with this dossier which suddenly had acquired for him the importance of a historical document, a coffer of marvels. He took a few more notes, then he returned the dossier to the Assistant Head with a ceremonious salutation, and went back to his own office. In the faces of the employees along the way he thought he noticed an unusual seriousness, though he had no time to think what it could have been due to. He was a bit overhwelmed by all that had happened to him since leaving his house that morning.

When he returned, the Sub-Assistant Supervisor had left, after putting away the portfolios that were on the chairs. The room did not seem the same to him, it seemed much larger, a hostile place that scarcely preserved a trace of what it had been throughout twenty-five years. To his eyes it was like a room in which a terrible misfortune had occurred: the same, but nonetheless somehow different.

He set to work. He had not thought about it before, but suddenly he recalled a conversation with another employee the previous day. He was brazen, a gambler, of the worst sort. Julio had gone to see him, and the other had explained in greatest detail a plan for the new government. They would rehire all those who had ever been dismissed. Employees who had for any reason committed offenses leading to their discharge would be automatically reemployed. Before that they would organize a demonstration, with flags, they would present a petition on parchment with gold medals and everything, and immediately a decree would come out nullifying all the dismissals. He calculated there must be about five hundred in that Ministry alone. There must be as many in the others. Maybe seven thousand demonstrators, with flags and speeches.

On the other hand, they would throw out all the employees appointed during the last ten years, without investigating a thing. To Julio, this seemed a colossal measure: an act of justice. He remembered all the details of the conversation, even the vocal inflections of his interlocutor. Just after that news, some distorted versions of it began to circulate, and the office filled with people. And moments ago now, he had just obtained confirmation. He could link those conversations with what had just happened to him. What Berdier had told him in Pita's presence, and the latter's servile acceptance of all Berdier's words, corroborated that prediction. Berdier was one of the scoundrels, and yet he presented himself as a secret agent; more, as a detective who was up-to-the-minute on a thousand little details, such as those of Julio's visitor and his errand trips outside. All this was very suspicious and puzzling.

He began his work. It was two-fifteen. He had an hour and a half to do the report and propose a settlement, with five carbons. He knew the affair quite well, and with Berdier's facts and admonitions everything was eased. It was necessary to search out the attenuating circumstances, declare certain previous proceedings defective, indicate the contradictions— which he had already annotated—and turn in the work. But his Supervisor—had he really been arrested and placed incommunicado? Julio was alone in the office, in shirt-sleeves. He turned on a fan. Gone from the tables were the dossiers, which were normally kept in cupboards, in boxes, and in the storeroom. Stacks of dossiers could be seen in their colored portfolios through the stippled glass panes of the cupboards. He had not had a bite to eat since breakfast. He had to finish by three-thirty at the latest. He would lose a few minutes talking with the Supervisor's secretary. Many of the things that had seemed strange to him had been made clear. Not one by one, but all together; he had the key now, and everything had lost its air of mystery. He was in a state of mind in which nothing could surprise or astonish him. Nothing. He set to work writing the first draft.

In the Main Office there was an unusual amount of movement. People were coming and going, entering and leaving. They were getting ready for the Confirmation Party (for the higher officials). It was said they would be coming in from other departments. Enormous bunches of flowers were brought in, cartons full of liquid refreshments, trays with crackers and sandwiches, dishes, cups, fruit bowls, ice cream, boxes of chocolates, baskets of *empanadas*, clusters of colored balloons for the children, and packages of whistles and paper streamers. The quantities were incredible. Workers from decorating firms were setting up wreathes, shields, and flags. Some of them, on ladders set on top of the furniture, were decorating the enormous reception room. It was a drawing-room fifty meters long, twenty wide, and at least ten meters high, with great bronze chandeliers covered in crystal fringes. The tapestried walls, the carved wood, the carpets on the floor, all were of imperial luxury and magnificence. In one hour it had to be completely arranged, everything ready for the party. The higher officials would be coming with their families, and dancers would even be brought in from the *corps de ballet* at the theatre. One orchestra of a hundred professional musicians, another of thirty, which would be placed in the adjoining hall, with all the doors between them opened. On the other side of it there was another equally spacious salon, which formed an angle with the former. The orchestras would be heard in both salons and in all the other offices, which were to remain open to each other with their doors wide open. From one of the salons, the one to the left, all the furniture was removed and the carpets taken up, and the floor quickly polished for dancing. The number of workers and office helpers engaged in the work was unbelievable. There were also some junior clerks who had asked to help out, because they would be paid twenty pesos for the work. They only had to work fast and without resting for an hour to earn what they would normally get in a day. They all worked without becoming annoyed, as if they were accustomed to doing this all the time. There was an invasion of porters, polishers, upholsterers, workers skilled in all the arts of ornamentation, florists, floor waxers.... Nievas worked without suspecting what was happening a few yards from his office. He only heard muffled noises, voices, footsteps; but they never attracted his attention. He was in a state of mind in which he found everything reasonable, natural. Neither did he have the time to inquire about anything. His task was no less urgent than that of the workers. He had to finish his work, with five copies, before three-thirty. By hurrying and using his notes and memory skillfully, he was able to put the papers into the typewriter even before finishing the first draft and begin to produce the report and its decision, editing and perfecting even as he was copying it. In reality he was bringing more to the final version from out of his mind than he was taking from his notes and drafts. Thus he finished the report and the resolution rather quickly, by three-fifteen.

When he got to the secretary's office, she was just returning. He explained that he had had the charge of handing in this affair before leaving. He asked if she would let him go in to place the dossier on the Director-General's desk. The secretary let out a noisy guffaw. Nievas was unaware that the office of the Director was now converted into a party room. She advised him to take it to the office of the Sub-Secretary, on the second floor.

A great many people were arriving. The elevators were filled, coming up as well as going down. He chose to use the stairway. There was no one in the office of the Sub-Secretary, not even the office boy. He walked along several hallways in search of someone whom he could ask. But he only found one soldier, with fixed bayonet, who did not know how to answer one word. In reality, he was unaware even of where he was. So that when Nievas asked him if the Sub-Director or Sub-Secretary was in, the soldier looked at him strangely, as if he had never heard that such a class of people existed. With the voluminous dossier in his hands, careful not to lose any pages, Julio decided to go back up and ask the secretary once more. Besides, he needed to know if his leave had been signed.

When he got there, the secretary's office was crammed with people. He approached her to ask about the thing that interested him most, his leave, and the secretary told him that yes, it was ready. And she handed him a copy of the memo informing him of it. As far as the dossier concerning the investigation went, she could give him no idea of what he ought to do. It was not the moment for that, either. Suddenly the one-hundred-musician orchestra was heard, playing a Strauss waltz. The music resonated with incredible force, as if the musicans were right there with them. The whole enormous building was vibrating like a box especially constructed to multiply the sounds.

Upon returning to his office with the dossier, Julio discovered the Sub-Assistant Supervisor, who had arrived a moment earlier, and with all his dossiers upon his desk was already working in his shirt-sleeves. He seemed not to have noticed the din.

"Do you realize...? What do you say to this?" he asked him, with the dossier held out like a tray on both hands. The Sub-Assistant Supervisor looked at him.

"Realize what? What am I supposed to tell you?" he asked in a voice as if nothing were happening.

"The uproar."

"Uproar? I don't know what you're referring to."

"Here is Berdier's dossier. Do I leave it with you?"

"Did Berdier talk with you?"

"Yes; he gave me some instructions before I took care of the file."

"I thought you had left without finishing the job."

"Impossible. But if I have missed the train to Mar del Plata!" he placed the dossier on the desk. "Are you going to check it over now?"

"Of course. I have to take it up to be signed as soon as possible. Do you know if the Director-General has arrived?"

"I think so, because there are already a lot of people. And the orchestra has begun to play. Didn't you realize that?"

"I believe I am not deaf. So you are going away?"

"Yes. As soon as you authorize me. I have already been informed about the leave. It finally got signed. My wife will be expecting me in the waiting room at the station. I told her to take the four o'clock train. It's three-thirty."

"Someone called asking for you about ten times. It must have been your wife."

"What do you mean, ten times? I only went out for a moment."

"It only seemed a moment to you. When I arrived, you still weren't here."

"Did she tell you she was my wife?"

"No. It just occurred to me. She asked if you had left, and I told her, yes. Do you want to find out first if the Director-General has arrived? But put on a coat, please; don't go out like that."

Julio had forgotten he was in shirt-sleeves. He put on his coat as he was going out. The doors of the offices were open, and the music was flowing through the doors like a torrent of sounds. It was funny to see so many people. As the secretary opened a door, he saw some people in the waiting room, and among them he seemed to recognize his wife and daughter. They were seated as if waiting. What? Would she have understood that she was to wait for him here, in *this* waiting room? He tried to enter, but the door remained shut and locked. A crowd of guests was pressed up against it, struggling to get into the party salon. He remained there without knowing what to do. He was perplexed. He managed to station himself against the door frame; from there he could see the whole salon, and, through a wide door hung with flowers, the orchestra. There was an infinity of women among the members of the crowd. They were laughing in the most shameless way and applauding enthusiastically. The tables were covered with cups, bottles, trays, flowers. Some busboys came in hurriedly and removed from a little table everything that was on it, leaving it bare. Moments later, to great acclamation, laughter, and applause, a child entered, identical to his daughter. Was it his daughter? Divested of her street dress, with hardly anything on but a slip and her dancing shoes she was set upon the table and, in time to the music which continued playing a waltz, she began to dance. It was incredible and marvelous. Julio felt pride and shame. He tried to break through the crowd and take his daughter out of there. But he could not move; he was nailed against the doorframe by elbows and bodies. He observed the scene which was becoming more and more animated. Everyone seemed drunk to him. The little girl was dancing with self-confidence, like a professional ballerina. Many military figures, who were embracing their ladies at the same time they raised their cups, were saluting the spectacle. Julio was making desperate efforts to enter, when an office boy managed to reach him.

"Mr. Nievas, it's three-forty. The Sub-Assistant Supervisor told me to inform you that someone has been calling you on the phone."

MARTA RIQUELME

The unpublished work of Marta Riquelme—the name was known to me, even familiar, I don't remember where I had read it—which the reader will find faithfully reproduced below and which is introduced to him by this prologue, was written by its author with the intention that it should come to the acquaintance of many people. I mean, that it should be published, and this is what I am doing now, obedient to her will and to the interestingness of the narrative. But I should give notice that Marta Riquelme is not a writer. I would almost say that she does not know how to write. The originals were handed to me by Dr. Arnaldo Orfila Reynal, who obtained them in his turn from a friend of the author with the recommendation that I should look them over and, in case I found them of consequence, publish them with a prologue, which is what I am writing now.

At this time I should record an unforeseen vicissitude with regard to the fate of the manuscript, which I myself, with total lack of precaution, carried to the printer. I would like to believe that everything has been the result of disorder in the offices of the publisher and by the foreman at the printshop, and I should declare that I am determined to work on the prologue even though I do not have the manuscript at hand (I know it from memory and can reconstruct the writing which I envision exactly as if I had it before my eyes). I fear that the manuscript has been abducted by the hand of someone in the family eager for it to disappear. But before anything else I need to explain what has happened, and I ask pardon from the reader if I depart somewhat from the usual manner of prologues. Because, in short, this is as much the personal unburdening of a troubled mind as it is a prologue, and the fact is that in the text there is a prediction, even down to almost insignificant details, concerning the fate she believed that manuscript might suffer. One would say that Marta Riquelme foresaw such difficulties in a state of prophetic clairvoyance. I don't believe in those supernatural or at least mysterious phenomena yet; but when it is a question of Marta Riquelme, what is there to doubt? The author often uses such expressions as "my destiny," "what inevitably will happen," "since it is inevitable that this should occur," "I will never be able to emerge from my grief by means of these *Memoirs* which I am writing for my consolation and also so that they will be known by other beings who may suffer as I do, etc."

In the meantime I continue proceedings to rescue the original from its unworthy possessors, I mean the family of Dr. Finderalte, since the physician himself has deceased. I am determined then to publish this prologue without any scruples in this respect, because I have had to initiate a lawsuit to gain lawful recovery of the *Memoirs*.

Although this is an episode extraneous to the text, it is not so insofar as it coincides in its semantics with the destiny of its author, and it even reflects a fearful aspect of her mysterious existence. She too was snatched from the world or removed from our earthly life, in a manner of saying, for it has been impossible for me to find her, living or dead.

Last week I went to the publishers and then to the printer several times without being able to find the typed manuscript copy, corrected by our tribunal in plenary session for the last time to avoid slips (too many of which appeared in spite of everything, unfortunately). At the publisher's office they gave me to understand they had not the remotest idea of the book; perhaps they were trying to avoid giving out any information or excuses about the manuscript. It is true that I had turned it over to the managing editor with the peremptory instruction that no one should be allowed to touch it or look at it. Moreover, on his word of honor, that the manuscript should pass through no other hands than his, the printshop manager's, the foreman's, and the linotypist's. The other employees were ignorant of the very existence of the work, and the managing editor had not said a word to anyone before embarking for the United States. I went to the printshop, as I said, no fewer than ten times—the reader will understand my situation and why I report on these details—until, after having interviewed each of the higher employees and then the junior ones, I even questioned the linotypists, one by one. It is undoubtable, I thought, that my instruction had been followed with excessive zeal. No one had any knowledge of the *Memoirs* of Marta Riquelme, nor of any book of the sort I described to them, but without letting them in on its contents too much, rather out of fear that they might divulge the names which figure in it. Finally I decided to force my way into the office of the technical director of the press without being announced. He was astonished, as if he did not recognize me.

"Excuse me," I said, "but I am tired of wandering around and wasting my time. I need to compare some passages in Marta Riquelme's book, *Memoirs of my Life*, from Purple Land Publishers. It's stupid for them to be hiding it from me, since I am the true responsible editor."

"Didn't you see the sign on the door?" he answered me gravely.

"No. It's disappeared. I came in because you have refused to receive me twenty times already."

"I didn't know that. No one told me anything."

"Do you recognize me?" I looked at him fixedly.

"Of course, Señor Martínez Estrada."

"And hasn't your secretary told you how many times I have called you on the phone?"

"No, she hasn't told me. But, now, is it true that the sign isn't there?"

"What I need to know is whether you will permit me to consult the manuscript."

"The manuscript..." he imitated me, making each syllable stand out, as I had done, though with unexpected affability. "First of all, to what manuscript do you refer?" He got up and drew near me with a friendly air.

"I told you already. The *Memoirs* of Marta Riquelme."

"Oh yes, I know. From Purple Land Publishers. But the fact is, my friend...," he gave me a friendly slap on the shoulder, "that you are clinging to a matter which I believe has been clarified rather well by Señor Fino. The very day he left here, we had a long conversation by phone, but I don't know who it was—think now, search your memory—who spoke to me in your name about the manuscript so that I would turn it over to him."

And he contemplated me as if I were hiding some secret.

"And what did you tell him?"

"That it was here."

"Here?"

"Yes, that it was here. Though not here in my office, understand me, I beg you, but here in the press. Start looking for it now.... It's like looking for a needle in a haystack."

"I look for it? I hope it's not lost."

I felt a mortal shiver down my spine. Three years of work, plus three months to get it typed up.

"It can't be lost, if it is true that you actually delivered it. But that's the printing business. Because I seemed to have understood, from what Señor Fino told me, that you were set to bring it here but never did so. Besides, don't forget that six other presses work for that publisher, aside from ours."

"But it was going to be typeset here, in your printshop."

"Señor Fino assumed that too. But who, then, did Señor Fino give the manuscript to for the purpose of bringing it here to the press? Because no one has given me anything."

"It's lost then! Holy God!"

"I wouldn't want to say that, don't get upset. I see that you are very disturbed and that you are not understanding me very well."

Exactly. But to return to the prologue, dear reader, as I have already said, I have had to transcribe from memory, without being able to collate it with that only copy of the typescript. I have lost all hope that it will ever be found. Although it would not be impossible that Señor Fino had inadvertently borne it away to the United States in his suitcase, since during those final confusing days on the eve of his departure, they tell me he was carrying it about in a briefcase underneath his arm, fearful that it might get away from him. So I must necessarily turn back to the hand-written manuscript, not to delay this work and to honor the loyalty I owe you, dear reader. To wait for Señor Fino's return to get this contretemps clarified exceeds the resistance of my nerves. In any case, I will obtain another copy of the original that we five put together, though for me it will be a rather difficult task. Presently those manuscripts are held by Limperalto, the experienced and well-known calligrapher and graphologist who aided us; he was desperately interested in carrying out a psychological study of the author through the examination of her handwriting. (I should give you warning that, in my judgment, he was mistaken in his arbitrary hypothesis that we were dealing with a case of reincarnation: Maria Baskirtseff. An extraordinary absurdity. It will never clear any of this mystery up, I'm sure of that. I have to tell him that as soon as I can talk with him. Limperalto is very sick just now.)

Meanwhile I visited my friend Dr. Orfila Reynal and threw myself into his arms, exhausted.

"You have to help me," I told him, "I'm desperate. We have lost the copy of the *Memoirs*."

He looked at me in wonderment, as if I had just given him news of some disaster.

"You've lost it?"

"In the press or at the publishers. We have to talk to the person who gave the originals to you, and you alone are acquainted with him: Marta Riquelme's friend."

"What are you talking about, please? Don't you remember that that friend died a year ago? I think you are rather disturbed."

"Yes, I certainly am. Then let's pay a visit to Marta Riquelme herself. It's impossible to go on this way. I need to speak with her and get her to help me reconstruct her *Memoirs*."

Dr. Orfila Reynal contemplated me very compassionately and without saying a word went to look for a glass of cool water which I drank down at one gulp.

But I must continue with the text.

The story is a little complicated, though because of many attending circumstances it seems to me it must be interesting to the reader; besides, a perfect understanding of those *Memoirs* would be very difficult if I did not explain some of its particulars, from which it must follow that the work is not complete without the explanations. It is necessary for me to give them, and thus what I have called a prologue amounts to no more than a preliminary notice. I say it again.

These memoirs which seem to have been written as the simple unburdening of a tormented soul evidently bore the intention that they should obtain wide diffusion and even fame. I still have not been able to find out with certainty if the originals were given by her to the friend who turned them over to Dr. Orfila Reynal (through whose hands they came into my possession), or if they were stolen from her. This last hypothesis is quite possible, for since we are dealing with a sensible woman from a well-known family, it seems odd that she would voluntarily hand over those papers which evidently reveal unusual intimacies with a frankness very seldom used in this kind of confidential writing, since it includes the actual names of people, many of them her close relations, that have had some participation in events so strange and dramatic. To this day, neither Dr. Orfila Reynal nor I have been able to discover any more information than the author herself gives; but there is not the slightest doubt, judging by the many inquiries which I need to relate, that that woman exists. Or, to speak more precisely, that she existed; that she is the author of these memoirs, and that the other persons named in them exist also. When we went in search of Don Antonio Gómez Santayana, who would have some information about the Riquelme family, they told us in Bolívar that he no longer lived in the town. They knew nothing about him nor did they know a single word about the story of La Magnolia. General opinion in the town was that such harmony and felicity had reigned there as riches and family affection alone bring about. Concerning Marta we found out absolutely nothing, and even if I had been able to speak with her, it would not have been possible to question her on fundamental points of her *Memoirs* since that would have established a very uncomfortable situation for the author in the bosom of her family and with her many connections in the community or city where they live or did live. I visited the house, which today has, as formerly, three patios, the last one a kind of paddock where the horses are. A shed, with the harvester combine described in the narrative, still remains legally entailed after twenty years, as a result of the family lawsuit. There are numerous hens there, bricks, and mountains of manure that they squander inconsiderately. The second patio, which is connected by a passage through an arch, is bordered all around by apartments. In the center is the well, with its pump and a dipper used by everyone. On the upper floor is the old dining room, the great kitchen (several families eat together yet), pantry, baths. All of the two-storied house is in rather good state of repair, and the first patio has a third floor with apartments built of wood and broad, covered corridors. There are several stairways, some of them spiral, and in this patio, in its very center is the lovely, grand magnolia tree.

The family rivalries still persist, following the lines of descent and the collaterals. There are eight branches, with a hundred and twenty persons. They are distributed among the two principal groups of buildings, and despite the discords, they have not gone so far as to separate and go away to live in different houses, since of the eight families there are five groups, and the three remaining ally themselves with those, forming common cause. In the city or community of Bolívar it is said that the magnolia tree keeps them from separating and that the lawsuit is now eighty-five years old without a verdict. I have been able to inform myself concerning several particulars not devoid of interest, for example, that the repairs of the house and pump are done by lot, and the taxes are paid by turns. There is no administrator, and the last one ceased those onerous functions thirty years ago. Some lawyers live now in the house itself, linked by family ties to the inhabitants that, in the majority, bear the name of Riquelme Andrada, and they form part of the family rather as parasites than as relatives. There are a great many children and many who are ill. Naturally vendors come and go constantly, but there is a lot of silence, for there to be so many people residing there.

I have found out that Marta's family, when she wrote her *Memoirs*, comprised her father, mother, two sisters—Margarita and María—and two brothers who in the *Memoirs* are only alluded to. The father seems to have been a pawnbroker. He got along badly with his wife who, according to perhaps whimsical versions, had been deceiving him for a long time with C____ (I will not say his name). Mario, who is an important figure in the narrative, was a bank employee, and he still is, but in another city; he had fallen in love with Margarita at the beginning, and later with Marta, according to the *Memoirs* (though it's not very clear). María loved another young man, as you will see. Marta tried to take her sisters' sweethearts away from them and in this, despite her childish years, she was a she-devil. That is why Margarita kills herself. Eventually the father drank too much. Uncle Antonio was the mother's brother: a vile person. Marta ennobles him, God knows for what evil reason, since he had raped a child once: an episode misrepresented in the *Memoirs*. Remember this consideration when you read the pertinent passage (p. 764). It is believed that he may have violated Marta as well and that he cohabited with her! He had separated from his wife, who still lives in the same building. Presently he works as a procurer. As far as Indalecio goes, I have met him; he was a luckless person, having been dismissed from the office staff of a retail store. His wife is a great deal younger than he and rather pretty. She gives room and board to several persons and occupies a room herself with them. I discovered a few days ago that Indalecio died when his clothing caught fire and he threw himself into a wardrobe to put out the flames. The furniture was burned, too. When the door to the room was opened, the charred body was found and on it a box of silver coins locked with a key.

There are facts which the manuscript does not record. For example:

The residents of La Magnolia got up a lawsuit against the grandfather, alleging property rights. As there were so many of them, the judicature fell into great confusion, and after eighty-one years the suit was in the same state with a hundred and six files as it was when it had two. In the trial for recovery lawyers from the capital participated, as well as others who joined in on behalf of the large family without being challenged since no one knew whose side they would take at the end. Instead they sought to win the fifteen plaintiffs over to themselves. All were living on the verge of open hostility, often coming to blows, especially the women, who remained at La Magnolia night and day and who tended to take reprisals on the children. Besides, remember that they never went out for fear that some fresh intruder would occupy their rooms. The supposed rape of the little daughter of the woman who is never named, and who must have been very closely related to Marta—a paternal aunt, it is believed—seems to have been one of those cases.

Now that I am determined to publish the book, all scruples are aside from the issue because the author assumes the responsibility for what she recounts and for any degree of veracity that the facts might have. For my part I made other investigations that I do not intend to relate here, because they could sew doubt or suspicion over even that degree of veracity. Finally, I turn to a more important topic.

Another interesting aspect of this adventure is the deciphering of the manuscript, and everything in it is so perverse that even the paper and ink would seem to have been put at the service of the evil spirits. The work of deciphering the handwriting or the logogriphs of that manuscript of nearly two thousand pages has been a task superior to human resources, and I would not have been able to realize it if the assistance and collaboration of a group of friends who, being as profoundly interested in the content of the manuscript as in the exercise of patience which the deciphering of it signified, had not given me support. Their collaboration has been heroic. For three years we have met almost nightly in committee, or better said, in seminar, to carry out this labor. Though in truth, on a great many of those nights the task, which might be prolonged until dawn, instead of having to do with the text would revolve about some interpretation or commentary that would occur to us and that took us to the very boundaries of metaphysics. What is certain is that we spent many nights playing chess. For when we were fatigued from the labor of classifying and deciphering, we took up the chessboard to distance ourselves from our preoccupations rather than for distraction. And thus it would happen that, when a piece was moved, instead of announcing the checkmate we would say, "We ought to consider 'buckle' instead of 'trembling'"; to which someone else would respond, blocking the mate with a bishop, "I was thinking of 'agitated'; it makes more sense."

It was an impossible handwriting, and that is why I said before that the author did not know how to write. Not only did her penmanship represent graphologically the infinite complications of the labyrinth of her soul, one of the most complex and diabolical known in the history of literature, but the symbols accumulated so indiscriminately and in very individual strokes of the pen, made the task so difficult as to convert it into the solving of riddles. The f, for example, the g, and the p are written with a stroke so similar that if one considered them in isolation, they could not be discriminated. And the most serious thing was that often to confuse one letter for another meant to completely change the word as well as the total meaning of the sentence. Aside from this, it is a "dissembling hand," perhaps written with the left hand or with the deliberate purpose to snarl interpretation, making reading difficult with gaps and ambiguities that inject unavoidable alternatives into decisive passages. And that is without counting the endless number of loose pages that could be placed in different locations without altering the logical order of the discourse, but of course they do the meaning, and this in fundamental ways. Other times we would stop in a kind of ecstasy, without saying a word, for whole hours, meditating on a phrase that was apparently absurd but that promised, once it was completely won over, revelations that would compensate for so much cavilling. As I observed earlier, for us—the five executors who formed that group of hermeneuts and translators of an unlikely language—it was a matter of a very enjoyable pastime on winter nights, but absolutely painful on those of summer, above all if one realizes that for the three years this task lasted, not one of us failed such obligations a single time. At the end our work became transformed into a mania, similar to a game or a habit of doing puzzles in which neither the solution nor what comes out of it is worth the work or the satisfaction that one's own imagination encounters in the discovery of the keys. It is very possible that this alone is its cardinal merit, so that in depriving the readers of the process of disposition, deduction, and adjustment, the work turns out to be something like a picture of a crossword puzzle where everything has already been put in its place.

In no way can I assure that the text of the 1,786 manuscript pages which forms the present book is actually what its author wrote. It is very possible that we have committed some of those errors, so common among philologists, which can alter the total conception of the work, above all if one keeps in mind that some key words, regularly those written more carelessly or under the most anguishing imprecision, were the most problematically legible. This does not mean that I am presenting here an apocryphal text, or that it suffers from such corruptions of word and meaning that the readers might fear they are reading a different work from the one its author wrote or corrupted on purpose. That is not so, not by a long shot. But some words employed at times with excessive license, and almost inappropriate to the language of women, if not exactly the ones she used, might at least alter the moral aspect of the work. With respect to the idea we might form about Marta, who might venture a judgment? Often the author arrives at the verge of the precipice of obscenity, but she just as often attains to the mystic consummation of the purest souls. The reader must have faith in the fact that the text offered here is literally the same as that which the author intended and wrote; or at least that it can include only certain inevitable errata in this interpretation of hieroglyphs; or that, in the worst of cases, by the unanimous consensus of my collaborators and myself, we have made supreme efforts to preserve literal fidelity. In short, if the text merits such objections, one should not continue reading. It would not have been possible to go to anyone, and in this case not even to the author herself, to assist us in our absurd task. To have consulted with her about particular words or equivocal phrases that were from one point of view simple, innocent thoughts and from another were satanic occurrences would not have answered to our problems. I know her soul sufficiently well to attest to that. She would simply have laughed, without answering. Or what is worse, she would have lied. So that her cooperation would have spoiled everything, on the chance that in an ecstasy of repentance and dignity she might not have opted for wrenching the manuscript from our hands and throwing it into the fire.

But let us return to the topic forsaken a moment ago. Difficulties were also offered in the fact that over some obscure passages we would initiate discussions about the multiple interpretations it was possible to give them until, after once having become familiar with the psychology of the author—and that was a delight, I must confess—and with the truly extraordinary facts of her life, even the most trivial sentence was enough to leave us in perplexity. Then we usually retired to the chessboard. For example: it astonished all five of us to find this declaration in the middle of the very first page: "I understand by my destiny that this book will never be published." Because as time went on, and with the incredible episodes that complicated the labor of typing up those pages (pages that were on the other hand in complete disarray and with some even placed so capriciously among the others that simply to order them and number them lost us nearly two months), we all reached the conviction that in effect this book would never be published and, more seriously yet, that we ourselves would never finish getting the loose sheets properly in order, would never read the text correctly, and would never come to an agreement in order to turn it over to the editor. But that is another topic, and very annoying, as I have mentioned with regard to the theft, loss, or destruction of the manuscript. Concerning subsequent events or, in line with the author's prediction, concerning what she understood about its being in accord with her destiny, it is better that no word be said, because if that prophetic sentence referred to the original manuscripts themselves, she was right. Further on I will relate in a few words some of the circumstances having to do with what I have already hinted at. I want now to continue with this species of obsession into which my collaborators and I had fallen, which consisted in bringing us to a halt to examine every phrase that seemed ambiguous or with a veiled meaning until we became enmeshed in disputatious arguments which, as a panorama of sophisms, intuitions, absurd and logical deductions, if they had been registered stenographically would not only constitute an important work in themselves but also would be of consummate interest for the total understanding of this extraordinary work. It will suffice for me to suggest as an example that the first paragraph with which these memoirs proclaim themselves, and which the reader might perhaps read at first without uneasiness—"Ah, my life!"—did not call our attention to it very much either when we first began our reading. But on page 40, where this exclamation and this sentence are repeated, there opened out suddenly a new meaning for us that was almost unfathomable. I understand that it is indispensable for me now to anticipate a little the content of the work which you are about to read, not with the intention of explaining it—that would be impossible, ridiculous—but as a simple, helpful guide on a trip through a marvelous country and full of perils and charm.

Marta Riquelme began to write her *Memoirs* at twelve years of age, in her words, as if she had awakened one morning in a strange bed, terrified. Although she does not indicate dates or the period of duration of these memoirs, by the events it may be supposed that they could not have comprised more than eight years. So that when she finished them, she would be reckoned as twenty, and at the present time she would be no more than twenty-four.[1] I make this remark because the sensation of time in the novel is deceitful. A reader little accustomed to such problems could assume that the memoirs embrace half a century, and from what the author tells on many of her pages, that she has reached old age. It isn't so. But that does not mean to suggest either that those eight years are not equivalent to an entire century, much less half, considering the intensity with which she has lived her life: now savoring it minutely, then as if she were shutting her eyes in a fit of vertigo. If the reader observes carefully, he will notice also that by the nature of the events, by the disposition of the figures, and by the thousands of details that will be perceived in the reading, time simply has no importance. Neither does place. I believe that the town of Bolívar is placid and with not a very large population. But if one forgets that these events took place there and in our own time, one might fall into the false conception that we are dealing with a city which is immense and of some far away time. Besides, explanation is lacking whether the author has not situated the action in Bolívar because of one of her habitual pranks. In synthesis, the argument can be expressed in a few words. So few, in fact, that it would run the risk of turning out to be nothing but a miserable caricature of a work that is the faithful portrait of so many lives. That from the time of her infancy Marta Riquelme has loved passionately, and that almost from the time of her babyhood this love has taken on the magnitude and the strength of a passion in the maturity of life, may be exact according to the reading of the book, and it may be false. Each reader will judge from his own experience. For example, to understand the situation of that precocious and troubled soul, in a great many cases it is indispensable to find the exact meaning of expressions that ordinarily are very ambiguous in her.

A major contribution to the reader's perplexity—and we spent a great deal of time in this state—is the frequent use of certain verbs, one above all that is quite pure and of noble descent although proscribed from our conversations. Is it that they used it when they talked in the Riquelme household? Or is it an affectation of language? Is it that under the pretext of being ignorant of its obscene signification she prefers it to another and to some degree especially when in its true sense it may induce to the most scandalous errors? How far her innocence and lack of knowledge about the world's coarse vulgarities go ... but I don't even want to think about it. The reader will judge, impartially if it is possible, when this verb is encountered in the text.

We all got to know the manuscript by heart, I better than any, we had poked around in it so much, commented on it, dissected, weighed, and turned it backwards and forwards, shown it against the light of all possible interpretations and in all the foreshortenings of its labyrinths and colorings. Nothing was hidden to us except that which—yes, the very thing which no one will be able to discover until the consummation of the centuries—she herself is certain she could explain no better. During the preparation of this prologue which I would have wished to limit to a presentation of the author and her work—or better said, of the extraordinary situation that both constitute—I needed to go back to the text in order to be sure of myself, but I could not obtain it. So that the transcribed passages that I interpolate here believing them indispensable and, as a rule, absolutely so, are done from memory, subject as such to venial errors, but at most of punctuation and never of meaning. I must bring up this fact at least to justify myself before the friends who collaborated with me for three years with such determined ardor. I should say something about this episode.

One of those expressions that perhaps may not surprise the reader but which plunged us into the most impassioned perplexity is this one from page 18: "I didn't want to. I would never have allowed my uncle to...." A sentence ambiguous in itself, but which the reader will find explained further on. This love, or this passion, of Marta Riquelme's was pinned to, in a manner of speaking, one of the personages in her memoirs: Mario. No one can doubt that. Just as her older sister's suicide had nothing to do with a story of common jealousy, either. The truth is something else. I have no authority to judge, and besides, this has been a point very much debated in our gatherings without our managing to come to an agreement. In the meantime, as the reader will observe in reading the text, Margarita's suicide has much more important, even noble motives which turn out to change things completely by raising serious doubts, not only about the kind of relationship that existed between Marta and Mario, but also about that sinister figure of the uncle, who was seen as a proper gentleman only by two of us. (See pages 76, 121 to 125, and 836ff.) On the other hand it is unquestionable that Mario's love for Marta acquired so dominating a power that it would not be hazardous to imagine that her supposed passion for him might be something else rather than the fascination exerted by that love within her innocent soul. The other case of incest, which she very delicately insinuates by means of evasive words, but which comes out unmistakably from the complete text, is quite clear. But I should observe that in the reading of the original, one word, only one word which might have been read in two distinct ways, would have been able to radically alter the repugnant significance of the episode in which Marta Riquelme tells of it. Her uncle does not appear with the same psychology further on. Still, the most serious obstacle is to admit that a young girl, we might even call her a child, since that episode is found almost at the beginning of her *Memoirs,* could have been able to be aware of such a dismally base affair which furthermore was so well dissembled by its protagonists and which, if we have interpreted her manuscript properly, only someone who has had long experience in life would have been able to bring to light. The sentence, "He was a charmer," which she employs referring to her uncle, like that other which begins a lengthy paragraph on page 118, "One day he seduced me," might serve as a key and also create an insolvable riddle. Although these isolated words and phrases do not hold the explanation of the events which it is legitimate to imagine, they suffice to create a very serious problem for the reader, for depending on his sensitivity they might incline him either to consider Marta and her uncle as perverse figures, or else to assume, with the candor that is indispensable in the reading of a work of this bitter purity, that she is totally ingenuous in her affections. Now, I can see that the reader has not participated in these lengthy discussions, and that perhaps I ought to have proceeded more methodically and commenced by telling something about the house, the family, and the many acquaintances that join in to have an integral part in this almost rural tragedy. Regarding the house that they all lived in together, the parents, the uncles with their respective families, Marta's brothers and sisters and cousins, plus that numerous retinue which periodically would come to visit them and who, though distant relatives, appear in her stories as strangers and even intruders, all that is minutely described by the author. It is not worth the trouble then that I should waste time here describing it, apart from the fact that I could never do it with the proper effect and the sense of reality that she succeeds in, as will be found in the text. Nonetheless, there are two passages that I need to emphasize among the many pages in which the house is described to the point that it becomes transformed not only into the womb of these numerous dramatic episodes, but into a personage that influences with its character, its architecture, the out-of-the-way place where it was built, and the aspects it assumed depending on the day and the hour—in fact, into the very protagonist of the story. The author says: "The house was a tragedy, and we only acted it out. In that house, no events could have occurred except those that did occur, nor could anyone have lived there except those that did." "The arrangement of the apartments, the enormous patio, where the annoying encounter between my sister María and Serafín took place that I perhaps prematurely told about, the gratings over the windows, the height of the wall, the color of the doors perhaps, were what made it impossible to live there without the sensation that something terrible would have to happen the following day." Or when she simply notes, "The springtime never penetrated into the house," a suggestion that she repeats almost at the end of her *Memoirs*: "The whole springtime was turning about the house, it was raging in light, in color, in fragrances, but it never penetrated inside."

I will point out some other passages that should be transcribed in this prologue to make them stand out from the text because of their explanatory meaning rather than for their literary value.

"Something I do not understand is that, since heaven has endowed me with as many graces and favors as a woman can desire, and with a certain intelligence besides, I should still have to be so unhappy. What use are they to me, this beauty of face and body, these mannerisms so refined that they set me apart from all the women I know, if they only awaken envy and attract enmity and make me suffer more than I enjoy? I do not have the benefits of the life that goes with the rights nature has granted me, and I am suffering, suffering, suffering in my flesh and in my spirit."

"I am always saying it, over and over again without tiring, almost in the very same words, that this gigantic magnolia tree in the middle of the main patio had a human personality, that it was a member of our family complete with great boughs, smaller branches, tiny leaves, with relatives from so far away that they could only be justified by the common trunk of their ancestors. For we also were linked by a remote origin and divided into numerous independent parts which nonetheless lacked the freedom to grow closer or to separate further, because of being bound to an invisible trunk."

"La Magnolia was an old colonial farm home that my great-grandfather built. It had at that time no fewer than fifteen apartments which, aside from the manor house still preserved, occupied a very large piece of land. All the relatives lived there, and the family was quite numerous, so that the house was always totally occupied. Later on, I have no idea when, more rooms were added and the three patios built which still exist, separated by an adobe wall that does not hinder a view of the rest of the farm from the upper rooms. That plot of land came to be situated in the center of town because lots were sold off and built upon until the town was formed, and later still, the city. If towns generally are formed by the overflow of people toward the surrounding areas, in our case the opposite happened: the environs were contracting, and finally the house came to be the whole town, summed up, condensed. Later you will see how that happened. It was my grandfather, a man now of mature age, who thought to convert the manor house into a hotel and he gave it the name 'La Magnolia' that everyone knows it by. The upper part dates from that period, built over the old walls, where the rooms for the guest lodgings were afterward located. In short, by the beginning of this century it already had seventy-two apartments, some of which we are living in now. Because it turned out that, aside from the extremely large family, the hotel was harboring very distant relations and some people who alleged some relationship that we never understood very well, with some of these intermarrying until they formed a net of new relationships over others that had disintegrated. When the hotel was completely occupied by members of the owner's family, my father decided to close out his business, and since then that great house, with its magnolia tree, has been the place we all live in but which we cannot leave. I attribute the fact that we are also rooted here to the personality of that tree, so powerful; and it is as absurd for any of us to get out and establish another home or try our luck away from here as it would be for a branch of the magnolia tree to break off by itself and go take root in another town. I have already told of my impressions as a little girl, on the clear nights of summer, when it was all covered with blossoms just like the sky full of stars, and the pleasure that I experienced beneath its extended boughs, touching the aged trunk through which it seemed to me I could sense a fragrant life coursing. I believe I have also mentioned earlier that the immense population of the house did not keep very friendly relations, nor did they behave as members of the same family should behave, either. But I ought to say, since I have not done so yet, that the amount of sympathy and affection was greatly inferior to the amount of rancor and aversion, so that one could say we remained united because we hated each other, as if we kept ourselves together by the prospect of seeing how our enemies were disappearing. At least that is what I thought I observed as a little girl, and also now that I am fifteen, when from the upper rooms of the third floor I would watch the other patios and the other apartments where there was always a world of people at their daily activities. But once a year, believe it or not, on the anniversary of my great-grandfather's wedding, the twentieth of February, we had a great party in which we all participated, and that day and night until the next dawn the whole house was filled with songs and laughter, we embraced each other, even those we hadn't spoken to during the rest of the year, and even though when the day of the twenty-first dawned, we would return to our ordinary life. I remember that this date often fell during Mardi Gras, and that we would celebrate the fiesta in costumes and disguises, the children as well as the adults, and that friends and strangers even came to it as if within that immense house, in those enormous patios, the whole carnival of the world were being celebrated. That episode that I told about my mother, which caused us such annoyance and her so many tears, happened precisely on a twentieth of February, the last day of carnival. I won't repeat it here, therefore. Naturally many people had to go out to take care of their jobs, but from what I remember no one ever left our house to remain outside it for more than a day. It was also disturbing when any of our neighbors in this small city died. At least three of those deaths were entailed in the history of the magnolia tree. One of them in a very special way, that of my sister Margarita, which I will tell about later on."

"The departure of Andrés, who was driven out by Uncle Antonio, weighed heavily on everyone, and on me as well despite the fact that such a conclusion was unavoidable for our tranquillity. What I have not been able to explain to myself is the violence with which Uncle Antonio proceeded in contrast with the calm attitude of my father. I can even assure you that at that moment I felt a great sympathy for Andrés and that it seemed to me we all had been very unjust to him. In truth, I preserve no recollection that I could call unpleasant; instead, in all conscience I must declare that in the whole matter I have been very influenced by the opinion of Uncle Antonio, whose infinite love for me is unquestionable, for he must have brought to light very efficacious reasons that I never dared to question. What is certain is that after that day, Mario's conduct changed noticeably, and if I had to determine when I began to notice that the amicable relationships between him, Margarita, and María changed, I would have to point to that date. It is natural, as I said, that my cousin Amelia was always very much in love with him and that the struggle which was set up between us was a struggle of pride over the conquest of a man whom in reality we only thought of as a trophy."

"We were really irritated that day, in each of the patios, though they did not let us witness the scene, we contrived to listen by gluing ourselves to the doors and windows which were hermetically sealed. Doña Dolores arrived in a fury clutching the hand of poor Camila, whom she was dragging along as she came. Her face showed great indignation, and the tears fell without her actually crying. We heard the whole conversation, which she kept ι p in a suffocated, animated tone. After three years, and despite my infinite investigations, I have never managed to convince myself that Uncle Antonio was the guilty one. I know very well that few loved him and that they found themselves disposed to any calumny, but in the long run it was dashed to pieces upon his immovable rectitude."

"My father still had not acquired the habit of drinking without moderation; without ever being extremely affectionate, he never gave us reasons to reproach him. The loss of his fortune in bad business deals—and not in gaming or vice, as was rumored among the families of the other patios—as well as Margarita's death, transformed him into a hateful person. Poor Mama! This conduct of my father's allowed me to become profoundly acquainted with the treasures of kindness and resignation hidden within her and that I had never suspected before. That misfortune added to many others in our home put into relief the moral figure of my mother in the foreground and relegated that of my father to the shadows, though he had occupied an important place until then. If we had not relied on the assistance of Uncle Antonio, our life would have been very arduous."

I should make it clear:

The situation with Uncle Antonio and his family was quite the opposite. Aunt Martha was a sick woman with a disagreeable temper who never understood her husband and quarreled with him for no reason except the simple pleasure of maintaining a poisonous atmosphere for everyone in the household. Her jealous fits were of the same sort as Margarita's; I mean, she was not jealous that her husband should be in love with another woman but because anyone else's happiness was odious to her.

I cite this reference from the beginning of the work:

He had left as Uncle Antonio had left before, disentangling himself from his family. Although Marta gives us to understand that Mario remained faithful to his promise of marriage, it would seem that her decision to accept him must have carried along with it other hidden motives. Note this paragraph toward the conclusion of the narrative: "It was only right, and a duty on my part, since Uncle Antonio had also sacrificed his home for me, that I should not behave myself in such a way as to add to his anguish. I was the only person who could encourage any ideals for living in him, and, as though he were deprived of any other protection, I felt myself attracted toward him with a tenderness more intense than I had experienced toward my own father."

As far as Marta's narrative art goes, I refer you to page 297, where she tells of a trip she made in the bus from Bolívar to La Plata. This is what it comes to, more or less:

"The bus used to make trips between a large city of the interior and the capital of the province [one infers that it went between Bolívar and La Plata]. All the seats were taken by passengers of different ages, classes, and behavior. Among them there was a fugitive from justice, but as everyone was keeping to their seats, it was difficult to pick him out. The bus left the station at 7:20, that is, at the exact time indicated on the time schedule. The first twenty kilometers offered nothing unusual that might attract anyone's attention, and what happened later on did not awaken the curiosity of any of the passengers either. A young, blond woman got to her feet and took off her blouse, remaining in just her skirt and undershirt, for the heat was beginning to be felt despite the open windows. A little later a man removed his shoes and put them overhead in the baggage rack which was occupied by suitcases, packages, and boxes. Some uneasiness might have been noticed among the passengers had there been some observer with sufficient impartiality to notice the process of the changes experienced on the journey. It's enough to say that—a strange feature—all the passengers, even the children, seemed to bear a soft down on their faces, like adolescents."

Also worthy of attention is the gallery of characters that parade through the *Memoirs,* as I have already hinted.

In the manuscript there occur exactly thirty-six names, and only four of these do not belong to persons important in the narrative. These are mentioned incidentally, without their figuring again later on. On the other hand, there are eight persons who are not named and who participate directly in the action; one of them is a decisive element in one of the most affecting episodes. That is the woman who is chatting in the room adjoining what the author calls the "Civil Record Office" of La Magnolia when she goes to complain about the violence committed on her little daughter. This woman, who is not named, is the same one who appears in other important scenes. For example, she is the one who tries to set fire to the third-floor rooms, which are built of wood, as a result of an altercation with one of the deliverymen; the one who, without putting a fence around them, plants peas in the patio where were kept the horses of the "invaders," as Marta calls them (though they were really tenants); and so on.

Marta attaches no more importance to the deaths than the births, despite the fact that many of them must really be considered as murders. Marta herself witnessed two of them. The death of Indalecio is in itself the most memorable of them—for Margarita's suicide, when she hanged herself from the magnolia tree which was all covered with Christmas candles and toys, stands out only because of that circumstance—and Marta tells of it in such minute detail that it makes one think her sadistic. Of course, her sister Margarita's suicide also, you will notice, is narrated with a wealth of detail and she even uses the words actually delivered on that occasion, as she is accustomed to whenever a scene has affected her. It is rather doubtful that those spectacles could have made a really great impression on her. Instead we must believe that she witnessed them in cold blood, perhaps habituated to violence by the atmosphere that reigned in that phalanstery. It cannot be denied that Marta provoked, or urged, or better yet, shoved Margarita into that extreme decision. For how else can one interpret that final dialogue between the two sisters, in which Marta says, "If you had had more decency, Mario would have kept visiting the house here instead of going to visit the cousins on the second floor, Front B. You shouldn't have survived your treachery"; to which Margarita responds, "I already know what you mean to say: that I should hang myself." "Let's see you do it." "You really want to see it?" "It would make me happy, if it turns out." Then is when Margarita unties the clothesline and with the clothing still dangling from it runs to the tree, climbs up, reaches a high place among the thick branches, and fastens one end of the rope there. Then she comes back, like a monkey (Marta says), climbs down, removes the clothing still attached to the rope, looks for a chair, and without saying another word, hangs herself. All this, as the reader will see, told with a wealth of details. It covers six pages (321-25), in which Marta shows off her best narrative style.

    Indalecio's death is something else again. I will transcribe the story—it appears as Appendix II to this prologue—for I know it by heart. And not only I, but all five of us decipherers knew it, and we would often tell it, taking turns or just in parts, it is so well done. In résumé: that morning Indalecio seemed as though his eyes were clouded over. It was in vain that he kept rubbing at them, for a kind of fog was filling the room. He was coming and going as if he were sleepwalking, wandering about attempting to dissipate the fog that was bewildering him. His wife was astonished upon entering the room, for she had the impression, despite her being so close to him, that he must have been a long way off. She heard his shouts and screams as if from a distance. She found out he was fixing up the bedroom of one of the neighbors on the second floor, Side A, where he normally went visiting about eleven. And so on and so on.... (Parenthetically, it seems a mockery here that Marta should say that Indalecio was a bigamist and that his second wife lived as a domestic for a man who was a corkworker.) There is one page written on paper of a larger size—legal size—that we have not been able to paginate. In the typed copy of the manuscript it is inserted between pages 422 and 423, because what precedes it and follows it would seem to indicate that that fragment ought to be interpolated there. It is not for certain, nevertheless, and the reasons for this are explained at the foot of that page. The author would have done very well to destroy it (and we would all have been better off if she had burned the whole manuscript, even though we would have lost a jewel of incalculable value). We spent three months attempting to place it into different passages where it also could have stayed and made good sense, often with valid reasons to prefer that to the other places. Further, it must be said that the suspicion was raised among us that this sheet, written on both sides in tiny letters and very clearly, must have been written on purpose to contrive an enigma. Provisionally, it was with other pages where it could not be fit in, unless the case were that it should have followed a paragraph in the middle of that section, where it likewise could have a corresponding sense. We discarded all the other possibilities.

The reader must have realized, after bearing in mind the integrity of the text, that depending on the location where it is interpolated, it alters even the meaning of the story she is telling about the personage it deals with. Suppression was unacceptable, since it was a matter of a passage of great inspiration, to call it thus, within the veracity of the text. But be advised that this page says nothing—it clarifies nothing—and nonetheless, how profound the upheaval it provokes depending on the place in which one reads it! One might say that it more than alters, it obfuscates the meaning of one of those "destinies," as Marta says of that charming person. Let the reader test it out by reading it first where it has been inserted and then reading it just after the sixth line of page 422; then after line 26 of page 105; and after line 9, page 14. In every case the text also harmonizes perfectly with what follows it in the succeeding paragraph. But with this difference: where it is now, it signifies that the theft of the wallet is due to the fact that Florindo was a gambler, he had contracted debts, and he found no better recourse than to penetrate the darkness of Indalecio's apartment and remove it from the writing case where he kept his salary and his savings. On page 422 it would indicate that it was by playing poker in a gambling joint that Florindo had won the fortune we see him with (without knowing how he got it) in that passage. On page 105, that it was he who with his financial assistance was able to rescue the poor girl who had come to ask for an emergency loan to prevent the auctioning off of some land her father owned; and on page 14 the passage would simply be an episode in the life of a prodigal young man, but it could just as well have been Florindo, which one infers that it was, as Mario. And with this, the idea of him that we have in the rest of the manuscript would alter completely.

How to interpret that equivocal scene of the wake?

The mother, with María and Margarita, goes out during the afternoon to find out if there is news at the Department commissary. They expect to return before nightfall. It is a very cold afternoon. They leave in a tilbury carriage. The car had been in the shed for three years because there were no parts for the carburetor. The hens were making their nests in its seats, and the rats had poked holes in its body. Uncle Antonio had promised to take them in a break he had borrowed. They didn't want to. At dinner time, Marta fixed the meal, expecting them. Uncle Antonio arrived to keep her company. She takes advantage of the time to unbosom herself of her sorrows. She begins to suspect that her father was a good person and that he has fled the house because he is fed up with the reproaches, just ones, perhaps, of her mother. Uncle Antonio then tells her a story of his youth, of his love affairs before his marriage, about his sweetheart and himself. He lies down on the matrimonial bed because he is cold. Marta brings the bedwarmer with coals left over from the meal. She sits down to listen. Antonio continues his story. It is ten o'clock. Marta lies down on her bed and leaves the nightstand lit. Her uncle begins to shiver, his teeth sounding like castanets. Marta goes to his bed to get him warm. She stretches out at his side, body to body. Impression. Antonio turns out the nightstand light and tells her another part of her father's story, rather fantastic, like a fairy tale. Marta is afraid, as much because of the story as because of her uncle. She throws her arms about him.

No less equivocal the occurrence of another incident, either.

Marta tells of her surrender to Mario. "I wasn't a little girl any longer." (Because she was sixteen, it is understood. Marta usually used the word "girl" in the sense of age.) She also says, "That period of my life in which the cloister had forbidden me more intense pleasures was over some years ago." (She refers here, as will be noticed, to her early childhood, and by "cloister" we must understand some period of time that she must have spent in the nuns' school which, according to what she says (page 12), she left when she was twelve. The period of the "cloister" must have been then, and the "more intense pleasures" are precisely those of her return to the house when her true conscious life begins, and her *Memoirs*.) These passages must be read consistently with Marta's innocence and purity. With this idea in mind, Mario's behavior appears to us culpable from every point of view; for it is natural that, after his having possessed her, as seems to issue from the literal text, she remained ignorant of the true significance of that act which, according to her own words, "brought her an indelible sign that in those moments she had been exalted by the angels."

Returning to the prologue, I am convinced that the misfortunes that are soaring like a raven above the rooftops and the heads of the residents and guests of La Magnolia are due to the influence of Marta Riquelme. She was a being born for another, better world, or for another ambience, if it were possible that there might be an atmosphere of love and innocence that could not be contaminated. It does not exist, I know that. Wherever she might have lived, she would have to have produced conflicts of the same nature around her as those the reader will find in these pages. Conflicts that one would say were generated by themselves, as if the life of the conflicts were independent of the life of the persons. Marta also felt that way: "The originators of the afflictions—she writes—are not those who take part actively but those who act passively; it is not the evil ones but the good people through whom the evil ones fulfill a destiny of things superior to human destinies." And in another place: "The house, La Magnolia, the apartments, the old furniture, above all the table service used by so many beings now gone, the shy servant girls, the insufficient lights, the perfume of the garden that faded as it penetrated into our rooms and our bodies. I myself, insofar as I belonged to the family of the house rather than to my parents' family."

She wrote this (page 526) at a high point in the story that makes one believe she must have been fourteen at the time. But with Marta Riquelme there is no time—I believe I have said that before—as there is no age for her body nor for her soul. At twelve she has the maturity of twenty and ultimately it is what she will have attained at eighty, if God condemns her to so long a life. Besides, this work is not a diary in which events are laid out chronologically, not anything like one. It is hastily written—with extreme urgency!—and the events can only be located with reference to the place they occupy in the general course of the action and to the pages in which they are found. Everything here is in disorder. The reader should not be heedless of the fact that the work begins with the exclamation, "Ah, my life!" And that this only acquires significance on page 686 where it is repeated in a logical situation, while at the beginning, what does it mean? I don't know whether I have already said anything about this. It is possible. Of course, it is just a kind of hook, and after reading those initial words, written in an admirable calligraphy, the reader—the decipherer of hieroglyphs—is irresistibly compelled to launch himself into reading onward until he is trapped in the net; and the more difficulties he finds, the more obstinately he persists. That happened to me. Neither the pages nor the events of the manuscript follow the order of the days or of logic. I have respected their order—I mean their disorder—but I understand that the reader will have to arrange each piece in its place, after a first reading, in order that the work can become organized and comprehensible. And then, how clear it is! For example, these sentences: "Disconsolate and with the impression that my body was ripped apart as if by the enlightenment of a confession spoken out loud with which our heart goes out of us. I didn't expect it of him, for I considered him, because of his age and because of the close relationship that united us, free of any baseness that might tarnish the love I entertained toward him as a valiant knight who rescues a poor captive maiden from the dragons" should go after "He himself understood the enormity of his offense. Was I guilty of provoking that cataclysm of his passions?" on page 325, where they seem to have a clarifying sense. When put before that point, where they are now, following the father's refusal to consent to her marriage to Mario under the pretext of her youth and the impoverished condition of a student who had no prospects whatsoever, they are confusing because they seem to refer to the father himself, when in reality they refer to her Uncle Antonio. Poor Marta never harbored such feelings toward her parents. At least, they cannot be inferred from her manuscript. There is no ill-will nor pity; instead there is comprehensive pardon. And nonetheless nothing exists in the remainder of the account, except the scene that followed Antonio's quarrel with her father and the brutal dismissal of Margarita—a veiled curse upon Marta's possible marriage and on her possible descendants—, there is nothing, I say, that authorizes one to think along those lines. To sum up, these vehement sentences are well placed where they are (page 1245), though they ought to be kept in mind in order to make the scene quoted from page 125 more intelligible; but if they were placed there, on the other hand, there would be no room for doubt about Uncle Antonio's blameworthy behavior. Even to suspect that is an atrocity.

Regarding the very rare occasions on which Mario is presented in the action—invoked, recalled, yes: many, too many times—it is done with incomparable mastery, if it were true that things did not occur in the way she narrates them. The slightest confusion in the events that preceded the presence of Mario in the dining room at siesta time, when Marta was embroidering a cluster of berries on a kerchief, would be sufficient for the nature of the relationship between her and her suitor to completely alter the moral situation of the two. Notice this phrase: "You must pardon me, Marta. I am ashamed." And her reply: she raised her needle and her celestial eyes at the same time: "Why? I enjoyed it too. I don't believe anyone saw us, and our pleasure has at least been intense, just what we wanted; and everything turned out lucky." This changes its meaning if it is placed after the scene in which Mario and Marta are alone at dusk, seated on a harvesting machine in the great shed—the one for the equipment—or after their flight into the garden where they picked the berries. In this episode Marta was singing a school song—as the reader will see when he reads the work—and a little afterward she exclaimed, taking

Mario by the hand, "No one sees us and no one hears us. I'm happy, and I feel I am alive in the same world where you are living. Of this scene of mystical happiness, with our hands wet from cutting berries, you and I, there will never be any witnesses, now or ever. I'm enjoying this silence and this solitude among the trees, with you. It is a pleasure I will never forget and I swear I will perpetuate these moments by embroidering you a cluster of berries on a kerchief. They will bring you luck." And she began to laugh, as she tells in her story. To place this dining room scene immediately following that of the harvesting machine would have given Marta's words a shocking meaning. But the passage is quite all right where one finds it now, which makes us think not of the writer's ability but of her truly limitless innocence.

It is maddening. It is agony and a torment to think how negligently this work has been fabricated—and written. It is quite evident that lack of skill on the part of the author, which led her to place observations outside their proper place and moment, permitting unverifiable suspicions to arise concerning her innocence and her life at La Magnolia, does not arise from the text, as we have already discussed to exhaustion and ended by discarding as a contemptible hypothesis; unless we should have to admit that ... but I will resist thinking about that, and I promise it now for the last time.

The text, as the reader will notice in reading the chapter entitled "Felicity and Shame," is that in which she tells of her most irritating struggles in the bosom of her family, without any other support than her uncle, who was decidedly on her side. That chapter from beginning to end is very ambiguous. There were great quarrels. Marta did not slacken and she faced her mother and her sisters María and Margarita with her inflexible character, determined to do anything. Her Uncle Antonio urged on her marriage to Mario, and thought Andrés should be removed from the house once and for all, particularly after his none too honorable slyness in pretending to court Margarita in order to pay attention to Marta. "It was a devoted love that my uncle went through on my behalf. I marked myself down as secure, and at the same time I doubted my strength. The love that I encountered in no one else, not even in him [she refers possibly to her father, judging by the page that precedes this episode], he offered me without stint, facing all risks including a final rupture with his family [for his attitude in defense of Marta set him up against his wife, the girl's parents, and nearly all their relatives. Marta's isolation is a real situation, not a supposition of her sensitiveness]. That afternoon we were alone in Margarita's bedroom, where occurred the struggle unto death that I told of earlier. Upon Margarita's departure with a howl of anger, I fell prostrate on her bed and began to weep. Uncle Antonio remained silent. I felt that I was completely abandoned and that only his presence there, his determination demonstrated on other occasions, gave me consolation. But I was unaware at that decisive and critical moment what attitude he might take. I felt afraid, because of all those circumstances that I have related several times before. If I strayed a single step outside the line that kept my loosened powers in balance, his support might represent a hopeless peril for me. My life, my destiny depended on his posture. If he opted unflinchingly for my defense by driving the one who was upsetting our old happiness out of the house forever, he alone could save me. I loved him too much to be able to demand any prudence from him. I felt from his silence that he was firmly determined to demolish the last barriers of convention in his love for me. As he drew close to me, I felt fear mixed with an increasing certainty that my situation would change with his help. I remained face downward on Margarita's bed, but I was no longer weeping. The struggle would be a terrible one, and if he decided it, my destiny could change that very afternoon, forever. I had no ties of affection with anyone except Mario, who at that moment did not count for anything at all among my confused ideas, and he held my fate in his hands. Would he defend me to the end, as I was hoping? Would he, by trampling under foot all feeling for conventional interests, allow his love to put the seal on an obligation which neither he nor I knew how long we could maintain? I felt myself seduced by sad, guilty thoughts. Everything depended on his attitude, and I had lost my firmness and, lying on the bed defenseless for the struggle, I would have no appeal to strength. My decision was that he should play the card of my destiny, without my hindering, without my remonstrations even. His position, if it were what I was hoping, would compromise no one but him. My love for Mario might slip into a secondary position, even vanish, in the face of the enslaving gratitude I would acquire toward him. He drew close to me and caressed my hair, without saying anything. My life depended on him. But could I, on my part, consent to a sacrifice so great? What happened then took on the magnitude of a major catastrophe. As if within us, him and me, forces of nature were struggling that we were incapable of controlling. From that critical moment everything would resolve itself in some manner beyond recall. My parents, the whole family would gossip about me, and an intolerable situation would be created for him, like his very existence. In burning combat on that hostile bed, like Isaac with the angel, my sentiments of duty were fighting with my passion, inflamed and also exacerbated by all that had been bothering me in recent days. Then he kissed me. I felt fire on my face, in my mouth."

And here is where appears the enigmatic passage: "I protected myself and at the same time I gave myself over to my destiny. My uncle seduced me // in that fiery bed with a virile energy that I never will forget // encircling me with his body and with his love in such isolation."

After many discussions, we five decided to leave it this way, for unless we might have read "bed" [lecho] where it said "struggle" [lucha], because the handwriting was more irregular in this chapter than in any other, there was no other interpretation. The reason for our doubts and for the heated discussions that lasted several days turned upon a line that in the manuscript seemed as if it had been interpolated after the paragraph was written, because of the little space that was left between the one paragraph and the other. It is this one: "encircling me with his body and with his love in such isolation." For if it were intended as an interpolation and was to have been placed where it appeared and not beneath the final line of the paragraph—as perhaps was the author's intention—that paragraph would be read this way:

"I protected myself and at the same time I gave myself over to my destiny // on encircling myself with his body and with his love in such isolation // in a burning struggle, with a virile energy I that never will forget." The paragraph, let us not forget, continues: "When those ineffable emotions were diminished, he told me: I will protect you against everyone. After what has happened, my duty to defend and protect you even with my life is the mandate of God. He was referring, I thought, to what had taken place in that gloomy apartment since the hour before, that is, since the argument with my father began and Margarita insulted me as she was going away, and all the rest."

This would, then, completely change the meaning and even the later direction of the *Memoirs*, for, as the reader will observe, they do not insist on this strange episode nor on the situation between Marta and her Uncle Antonio. Everything is resolved in the long run with the latter deciding to go against Marta's intentions by defending her; with Andrés being thrown out forever by her father and his brothers, although Uncle Antonio's situation becomes so difficult that he also resolves to quit this infernal ancestral house, alone, in an unexpected rupture with his family. In fact, just as Marta, with her infallible perceptiveness, had foreseen.

But neither are the words of the author explanatory. Instead they augment the confusion. That paragraph, which the reader will discover neatly typeset in the printed work, is one of the most entangled ones to decipher in the manuscript, since it contains crossouts over crossouts, words in the margin without any exact indication about where they were to be put in ("from then on," "threat of being obliged," "the certainty of blame and"). "He had lost his battle to win mine for me, and there remained with me, with his absence from then on, a motive for gratitude as well as of remorse since, as I thought a thousand times afterward, I should not have given myself over so stupidly to an action that it was within my duty, if not my power, to avoid, inasmuch as, freed now from the threat of being obliged to marry Andrés, there not only remained the love of Mario that I was still to fight for with spiteful Margarita, but also with María, who, as I have already said, was obsessed with distancing herself from me, with my having because of that separation to suffer the certainty of blame and even of a guilt impossible to atone for even with my detestable life."

A paragraph unbecoming, as one can easily see, the often inimitable prose of Marta Riquelme, though very much of her temperament, when the emotion rises within her to the point of obscuring her reasoning or elevating it to the spheres of the most glorious poetry.

Passion. Emotion. Often I have set those words down almost at random, and perhaps I may need to explain their scope. By "passion" we ought to understand, in Marta, the same blind and instinctive force that exists in all passion, although despoiled of its impure smokey aura. Marta has no experience with life, as the reader will observe reading her *Memoirs*, but from the beginning of her childhood, passion is a devouring fire that burns equally in her heart and in her brain. She simply establishes her personal experience and lays herself open to the inevitable tendency of every human being (much more so in the role of reader), for she can obscure the intensity of that fire by stoking it with her own foulnesses until she makes it flicker and smoke. She possesses without a doubt an almost inexhaustible capacity for love, but she approaches people and things with the candor of a virginal soul, she surrenders herself as if naked because she is ignorant of what we know. Her world is something distinct from ours and from that of those around her (in that, the origin of her tragedy). Besides, life in her home, that species of community that she describes to us so well, with nightmarish touches, is encompassed by, impregnated with impure passions, self-interest, hatred, and love at once material, terrestrial, egotistic, irrational. Only the self-denying, knightly figure of her Uncle Antonio is excepted from that judgment of "involuntarily wicked beings" which she applies to them.

So that this book, which is to be read, I hope, with passionate interest, has two texts equally logical and just: one in which Marta can be seen as I believe she is (the opinion of the "circle" of "exegetes" as we called ourselves remained irreconcilably divided in this respect), or as a feminine Satan that corrupts and destroys everything. A thousand times I wondered if the latter were not the truth; but a thousand and one times I thought not, hence my absolute verdict: final. I don't think about it any more.

Marta's passions, then, are those of a little girl, of a woman, of an old lady, even of men too, but she lacks sin, or sinfulness, to make it more precise. She loves, she dislikes, struggles with herself, expresses herself on occasions with a freedom of ideas and even words that surprises, but—doesn't innocence frequently nibble away at the harshest and most offensive themes, the most sensitive points of moral prohibition?

To judge Marta's soul, the examination of her emotions, always so spontaneous and generous, just as a psychologist would do it, turns out to be of useful assistance. Everything touches her and inclines her toward love. After the avalanche that sometimes spins her around and then sets her back on her feet, that tranquil kindliness which illuminates everything about her is reborn again. Her sensitiveness is almost sickly, I admit it, without falling into puerility. She keeps herself secure and dominates her emotions with the perfect art of an actress, or to be more correct, with her lack of a soiled conscience. This is evident in Chapters 8, 12, 19, and 32, true masterworks of description concerning her states of mind, where she attains the pathos of music. Neither should we think of anything Freudian. That was a hypothesis which, after it had obsessed us for more than a year, we all cast aside shamed and determined. Aside from the fact that we would have to admit that with an understanding of Freud's works themselves she might have constructed a formidable and unheard-of fantasy of her life, blurring the most sacred and the most vile things through allusions with double, even triple meanings. No, it is not possible to allow such a monstrosity, which would come to complicate a problem that in its own right is already inconceivably complicated. Freudian ideas are rooted in the distrust of the reader, I can assure you; and from my understanding of the most recondite secrets of Marta's soul, which I gained during the three whole years I consecrated to unravelling that awful calligraphy of a spiritualist medium, and from my eagerness to understand, I can swear that it is not ͛ɔ. What might be admitted is that the kindliness, the innocence, the chastity are Freudian insofar as the mind "like an instrument of exegesis and as a deforming lens of reality" can distort, debase, or sanctify everything equally. But his is a problem altogether foreign to the theme of this prologue, which only has as its object to explain some aspects of the text that will be read afterward.

I know now that there is a third aspect through which the work can be embraced, a "third reading" and even the most interesting; but to do so would oblige us to express Marta to ourselves as an hysteric—or as a depraved person—which is almost a sacrilege in the face of her luminous, angelic figure. Let it be inferred whether this is not so from the following passage of immaculate innocence: "I hugged her, my heart bursting with desires, I kissed her strongly on the lips. For a long time I had been hoping for a day like this; to possess her and enjoy her entire, exclusively. I kissed her, I kissed her. Because the words that had just issued from her mouth were worthy of the seraphim, and my anxiousness to go to the linden forest that afternoon constituted the height of joy which is granted to human beings only at rare moments of their lives. I desired to go, I wanted to realize, as in a vow, my dream of watching that gilded and calm evening fall like a canticle of God over nature. I needed it, like water for my thirst. So that for me, my mother, pronouncing those words which revealed her as in my own state of supernatural fervor, was like the being from whom in actuality I had received the best part of my soul. It was my mother that I was feeling within me."

Any equivocal impression apparent at the beginning of this marvelous description becomes purified by the waters of expiation; and thus it is, hundreds of times.

I ought to insist, in the face of these many difficulties, that the reader should not add anything to a literal reading, and that he should allow himself to be carried along by it as if on the wings of a Bird of Paradise, if he can. For if he is not capable of extricating himself from its possibly sinful insinuations, through imagination rather than sensibility, the best thing for him to do is to toss this book away right now, and never read it . He will merely find in it all the sorts of aberration that an impure soul is capable of.

The *Memoirs* conclude with a gesture that, in my opinion, shows a masterly hand. I anticipate for the reader, in order to alleviate the heaviness that I suspect will accompany him throughout the whole reading of the work: "As far as La Magnolia goes, upon my final departure forever it simply crumbled, it dissolved in the mist. I was turning my back on a pantheon full of burial crypts. It was inevitable, because destiny wanted it so, that I should go in search of my Uncle Antonio. He was also living in isolation, rent from the bosom of his family, the same as I. I was alone, absolutely alone in the world. At the right opportunity he was the sword that would defend me. I assumed his love would not have changed, just as my love for him had increased and glowed in his absence. Now he would have to be a fortress on my behalf who would shelter me against the recent reverses of my dismal life. My mission would be to console him as best as I could with my faint powers and through the help of God."

Everything that follows is simply stupendous.

[1] This prologue was begun in 1942 [Author's Note].

EXAMINATION WITHOUT HONOR

He did not intend to visit his supervisor, but he went. More precisely, he had been thinking about going; he had been settled on it since the night before, due to the way his supervisor had received him during the afternoon—unusually affectionately, considering his normal behavior, and brimming with flattery, which was irreconcilable, in short, with the temperament and mode of being he had always shown him in the Company offices.

The morning was of an obfuscating brilliance from sky to pavement, and never had things blazed with such a clear, pure light. A subtle atmosphere that seemed to be lifting him up surrounded him, inviting him to walk and to sing. As if the world were his, as if during the night every shred of squalor had been swept from streets, things, and souls, and now the city would rise in the dawn under a new sign of joy and happiness.

Without intending to visit his supervisor or go anywhere in particular, Cireneo began to walk, and inadvertently he climbed onto a streetcar that would be going past the hospital where he had been the previous day, visiting his boss, who was confined by a sudden illness. He got into the streetcar and experienced a certain well-being, the pleasure of a child on the way to a party—to the circus, let's say. The streetcar was also going along happily, at full tilt, without stops or jerky starts. People and things seemed endowed with singular immaculateness and clarity. Without a doubt something had happened somewhere on earth or in the heavens. His spirit was possibly what had changed, away from its natural disposition toward irritation and boredom. He felt himself rejuvenated, free of preoccupations, floating along in a streetcar that in its turn was floating on waves of stimulating light. He was settled on visiting his boss, therefore, without considering it further, he had installed himself next to the window of the coach that was sliding along without vibration. He looked with an old, youthful curiosity at the streets, shops, pedestrians, trees, vehicles passing rapidly by. It was a morning very similar to the one on which he had arrived in Buenos Aires from a town in the provinces, when his eyes, his ears, all his body, were opened to the astonishment of a new world. This morning was that same sort; he, too, was repeating himself. Even the idea of greeting his supervisor, confined for more than a week now, still flat on his back from some ailment Cireneo was ignorant of, seemed pleasant to him.

The previous day, nevertheless, he had had to overcome a very intense inner resistance, and when he left the hospital just as night was falling, he intended not to return. His supervisor had treated him with unusual cordiality, inviting him to try a few bites of the dinner which the employees of the establishment had served him. All were looking at him in a kindly manner, and even his supervisor was in a jovial humor, relating some anecdotes that were entertaining and at the same time annoying because they did not seem sincere. At any rate, it was strange, extremely strange: his boss's behavior, his pretended interest in talking to him of the possibility of getting rid of his office boy's uniform and moving up to the desks, through some miniscule efforts on his part; and above all, the fact that he would talk about his family and things that neither interested Cireneo nor belonged on the plane of relationships between superior and subordinate.

At the hospital corner he got down from the streetcar and looked around him, determined to enter. In the background through the broad entrance portal he discerned the tall, recently constructed buildings, white and resplendent under the blue, cloudless sky. In the morning light the hospital was something rather different from how it had seemed to him at the close of afternoon the previous day, when he had entered with embarrassment and in order to fulfill an unpleasant duty. Now it was nothing like that, just the opposite.

There was a lot of commotion in the office where the entrance cards were issued. Much too much of it for an admissions office of a hospital where so many beings were confined or were suffering, and where the souls of the patients as well as the persons accompanying or visiting them were so unhappy. The clerks, among them three women, but all in white smocks, were arguing vigorously though without actually shouting. They gesticulated and flailed their arms about briskly, their voices surprisingly subdued except when some occurrence drew forth a spontaneous and uncontainable laughter. They were gathered among the tables and desks around one of their number who acted as the center for the zestful conversation, and some were even sitting on the desk itself or were draped over it in order to get closer. Cireneo Suárez waited behind the counter. He was not in any hurry, and such an orderly liveliness even pleased him. From time to time the clerks broke off as if they were afraid their superior would surprise them in those get-togethers; they would walk around somewhat nervously and, pretending to be searching for some book or other, some file, they would form into groups again as if they had found unexpected reasons for continuing the discussion. He alone was outside this game, totally unaware, leaning against the counter on which were prescription pads, cards, inkwells, and some very large books just like those used for bookkeeping at the company where he worked. They were furtively playing toddle-top.

At length an employee inquired in a caustic tone, "Visiting or operation, Mr. Suárez?"

It surprised him that they would call him by his surname, since he had been there only once before, yesterday, and this employee had not been among the nurses who were doing things for and showering attentions upon his supervisor.

Suárez didn't understand the question and answered,

The clerk turned to the group from which she had detached herself and spoke to them without his managing to catch what she was saying; the others looked at Suárez with curiosity and joined their heads together again to go on with their previous discussion. They gave her a green card which the clerk filled out after consulting a metal card file.

"Next time you have to get here earlier. It's ten-forty. Understand?"

"I've been here for half an hour."

"You forget that it's necessary to be punctual. Take this."

On the card were all his personal details: given name (*Cere*neo instead of *Cir*eneo), surname, age, civil status, nationality, profession, the number of his military enlistment notebook, address. The clerks continued with their dispute, and now no less than half a dozen people were waiting as he had. He found it odd that his individual marks of identification were recorded on that card, without a mistake, and that on the back it should say: "Recommendation of the manager of the Juvencia Insurance Company, explanations, diagnosis and analysis a *posteriori,* Dr. Lancaster." He showed the card to the doorkeeper, who allowed him to go through to a broad avenue of poplars and linden trees, where there were patients on numerous benches with their feet, hands, or head in bandages, along with persons who were conversing with them, and clerks. Behind and to the sides were the flower beds, well-cared for and adorned with blooms. It seemed like a garden. Cireneo found himself perplexed, and while he advanced along the avenue he looked at the green card once more. He recalled now that when he was in his supervisor's hospital room, the latter had invited him to sit down on the edge of the bed, and when the doctor, the intern, and the nurse arrived, he had urged them to observe his friend and said to them—these were his words: "Without some significant ablation, I couldn't change his destiny." And he added, "Here he is, gentlemen"—and reddened as if he had committed some indiscretion or impertinence. Cireneo was dumbfounded; the doctor and the intern invited him to remain seated, and they began to talk about topics which did not clarify those enigmatic words of his boss. The intern kept walking around the bed and stopped at its foot as if to consult the temperature logbook, and he directed some words of a technical nature to the doctor; the latter answered him with affirmative or negative movements of his head. The nurse stayed in the doorway with a cluster of thermometers in the pocket of her apron, over her exaggerated chest. That was all.

Once more he looked at the card, which was perforated at the point corresponding to the date—twelve—where the doorkeeper had applied his train conductor's paper punch, and he kept on walking along the central pathway, surrounded by flowers and patients. He did not clearly remember the location of the pavilion where his supervisor was lodged, since from this point several paths split apart fanwise in several directions. He turned around to ask the doorkeeper and noticed that the latter was motioning to him irritably as if he had been pointing toward the right way for some time. He had to turn to the left, that was clear, but even after the doorkeeper's fingers had made a number of signals, he still did not understand them. He looked more closely and distinguished three fingers, and also that with his hand the doorkeeper was pointing first to the left and then to the right. That is how he went, turning into the third of five paths which opened out like a fan and each of which, thirty yards further on, led to the main corridor of one of the several sections of the first wing of the most important building. Behind it were the new buildings which were no longer able to be seen. He encountered some patients who went past hurriedly with little metal boxes on trays that shone in the sun. Down the path a patient on crutches, his leg bandaged to the knee, advanced slowly toward him. The man stopped in front of Cireneo and greeted him, touching the crown of his hat. Cireneo did not recognize him and continued on his course since he really had never seen him before. He walked a few steps and, turning around, he saw that the crippled patient had also turned and was saluting him, his hand raised. Just a question, he thought, of one of those patients who think they have really accomplished some marvelous feat if the doctor has removed a finger or cured an infection; he had probably got him confused with someone else, and it was quite possible that this was the reason for the whole series of misunderstandings which had occurred since the afternoon before. Although the green card he was carrying in his hand was conclusive; all the information and data on it were exact. Besides, he was wearing the uniform of an office boy, gray with flat metal buttons which today were shining so brightly that they irritated him, and no one else had taken off his hat upon meeting him nor shown even a passer-by's friendliness, not even the patients on crutches.

That left wing of the hospital was new. The hospital had thirty-five clusters of buildings, some of them raised when the hospital had been founded fifty years previously, others during different epochs, but all of them without a uniform architectural plan; since throughout so many years and so many directors, the original project, which kept broadening out with the years and the resources, changed in no less than fifty ways. The large gardens, which lay between the sections with their wards, laboratories, clinics, solariums, kitchens, storerooms, dining halls, etc., had never changed place; that is, those spaces had figured as gardens in the original plan, fifty years old, and as gardens they remained. The rest would not have been recognized by the directors, architects, and officials who had participated in the alterations and modifications. This part of the section to the left, or to use the language of the hospital, the Southwest Flank, North Face, Three, was relatively new. It had twelve floors, and the sun fell on one of its walls all morning long. Against that wall and along the covered corridor which went all the way around the pavilion there were many barrels of lime, piles of sand, some furniture which had been removed from the floors under repair, and scaffolding. One part of the building was complete, another under construction, and the third being renovated in order to set up some wards in place of the individual rooms which had been planned at the start of the work. So many bricklayers' tools piled up there rather gave the impression that something disastrous must have occurred, that the furniture must have been thrown down from the upper floors, and that a portion of the building had collapsed. But more closely observed, such lack of order did not hold sway; instead, things were placed about as they are when one works with them, not when they are packed up ready to be carried off. The operation was in full swing, though at that time of day no workers were to be seen around there.

It was nocturnal work. They worked at night in order not to disturb the activity of the hospital's other employees, whose tasks required them to pass close by, to occupy the elevators, to be calm without being concerned that the bricklayers' stares were fixed upon them, constantly on the alert for some carelessness in opening and shutting the doors and windows in order to witness some operation, or simply the transporting of the sick and injured on stretchers. The bricklayers worked at night with the result that they accomplished more and at the same time were not disturbing anything. They did everything discreetly and quietly, so as not to bother the sleeping patients, above all the many who, whether by the nature of their illnesses or through their state of groundless excitement, wouldn't shut their eyes if they became aware of the bricklayers lugging their pails of mortar or carrying materials up on the lift, or whistling—a habit they very soon lost. There were no bricklayers, I repeat, in the gardens, on the pathways, nor in the corridors, because they worked at night. These were also examination days—twelve thousand students were taking examinations during those two weeks in December—and neither was there any movement of students to be seen. They were all in the wards, the consultation booths, the dissecting rooms, the surgery amphitheaters, the lecture halls, the laboratories.

To the right there arose the enormous surgery pavilion, eight floors high, with great windows of polished glass. From a door at the side like a service door a man emerged, then another, and another, until there were six of them. Each was carrying a thick pole over his shoulder, like the strolling fish vendors, and from the end of every one there hung a complete set of inner organs: heart, trachea, liver, and lungs. Behind each of the men, to the rear and all sides of them, there sallied forth about two hundred cats of all colors and sizes. Men and animals walked along in silence. The orderlies wore striped blouses, pants of duck, and wooden clogs. They came from the storeroom. Every day they slaughtered eight to ten head of beef for the provisioning of the patients, the professional and administrative employees, and the inhabitants of the hospital. They would carry the entrails to a place where these were cut into pieces and given to the cats to eat. The latter were so accustomed to the job and the time schedule that they did not fight over their prizes, nor scurry about, nor meow while begging for their daily bread. They knew that there was always more than enough and that those who were in too much of a hurry might, as punishment, be debarred from eating.

A patient explained:

"They care for them and feed them so they will hunt the rats. This place is honeycombed with holes, tunnels, and fantastic burrows. Two buildings larger than these had to be torn down because they were falling down by themselves from the holes the rats made in the floor. They had dug cellars as large as four by four. So that's why. They have some wild battles with the cats at night. Beforehand the hospital staff make bets with the patients. Everyone gambles here. You can hear the howling for ten blocks. The rats howl the same as the cats, and there are a lot of them as big as dogs. They eat each other. In the morning you don't even see a body because the rats eat their own dead companions, just as they eat the cats. But there are some nights when as many as twenty die on each side. The rats are more experienced. Everyone comes to watch the battles, and some of the doctors bring chairs. It's wild."

Cireneo paid no great amount of attention to the patient's tale but remained as if rooted to the ground. Everything was very well organized in the hospital, according to his informant, above all since the triumph of the revolution's blue and violet list. In front of him was the maternity pavilion, ten stories high. One part of it, the upper, was painted. A scaffolding of about fifteen yards long was hanging before it. According to what the patient told Suárez, a woman painter from Honduras aided by nine Guatemalan painters was decorating an enormous facade on that wall, where the sun never shone. They were going to paint the symbol of maternity on it; the patient was unaware what it consisted of, although when he was speaking to Cireneo about this he winked one eye very seriously. The painter was a specialist in allegories, symbols, and emblems of all kinds, and she had already decorated more than a score of hospitals in North America. Here she had carte blanche to let her imagination express itself with complete freedom. The painters worked one or two days every week, since they all had other decorating jobs commissioned by the government.

In one ample courtyard, surrounded by an unplastered brick wall, many small flower beds, and a ring of privet hedge close to the wall, there were several tall poles with wires that could be stretched between them by means of pulleys, as if to hang out the clothes to dry. The place looked like a field for physical exercises and gymnastic games for children, one from which the slides and baby carriages had been withdrawn; or also, like a small-town cemetery. It was not the hospital laundry that was hung out on those lines, as it had seemed to Cireneo at first sight. No, they were assigned to patients who were following a new treatment, masterfully devised by the Assistant Director. These were hung from hooks with leather straps tied beneath their arms, and once the wires were stretched taut there was a gap of nearly three yards between their feet and the ground. They were dressed full-length in clothing of different colors—violet, lilac, yellow, gray, Nile green, sky blue—depending on their illnesses and the kind of solar rays it was desired to filter out. From a distance, since their suspended bodies stood out against the brick walls, they really looked like clothing hung out to dry, and that caused Cireneo's erroneous judgment. The patients of the solarium-aerium, as the place was called, did not find themselves made uncomfortable in that position, and as long as they had to stay there anywhere from nineteen minutes to three hours thirty-two minutes, they were allowed to read; thus some of them were hoisted up with their newspapers or books, and there was no lack of those more tidy folk who would bring along their handbag kits and take care of their nails while aloft. When Cireneo traversed the patio—and he did this unaware of the regulations of Section 4(M)—he caught the attention of the patients, who let their newspapers and books droop in their hands, some of them whispering to the others in tones of surprise and annoyance. Surely they must have assumed that the visitor was amusing himself by watching them from down below, which of course was not Cireneo's intention. Women and men alike, the patients tossed about, suspended from their clothes rack—that's what they called the straps with the hook that supported them from the wires. One of them asked him, "Are you an inspector?" Cireneo answered immediately, as if he had the reply already thought out, "Yes sir, an inspector from the Party."

At this point two nurses arrived with a nickel-plated pole based on a tripod, with a lever for unhooking the patients who had now received their quota of filtered solar rays. They were removing a rather obese woman with a sky-blue tunic. One of the nurses consulted her wrist watch and said, "Now!" Immediately the descent was brought about, by means of the lever that permitted the pole, with some sections telescoping into others, to shorten itself until the patient set foot on the ground and went off running to her room. The nurses went back again with their pole, since they were not permitted to remain longer than the shortest possible time to bring down the heliopneumatics, as that sort of patient was called. Cireneo also left and encountered three teams of nurses with their nickel-plated poles next to the door which linked the pavilions to the patio, each one under the direction of a supervisor who had a list in his hand and consulted his wrist watch from time to time.

Cireneo Suárez was lost. He recalled the doorkeeper's signals: toward the left, then down the third path to the right. That's exactly where he was. But this was not where he had gone the previous afternoon. Absolutely not. It didn't even look like the same place, with its vast gardens and the cluster of bungalows huddled together to one side spanning the avenue which separated this group of buildings from those of the hospital proper. He decided to go back and make certain. Had he come in from Marshal Gallino Street he would have been able to consult the plan or map at the gate, on which all the thirty-five clusters of buildings were located, with directions, letters, and a reference key for each one, for the gardens, and for all the housing—private, official, and temporary. Entering from Captain Ardite Street, there were no plans, no maps. He would have to consult with the doorkeeper or the caretakers.

When he approached the doorway at the entrance, the doorkeeper, who came out of his little box with its tiny window from which he had been watching him advance, pointed out the way again to him with gestures, this time overexcitedly. It was to the left, taking the third path, and afterward to the right. Yes, just as he had said before. But he added that Cireneo should go in along the corridor, and then he should knock. The route he had taken was right, then; it had only lacked the addition that he was to follow the corridor and knock, without which he could have gotten lost and wandered around the same group of buildings all day. Just a case of an omission—or of a trap, he thought, because as a doorkeeper who has no other mission than to punch the cards and show the right way to each recent arrival, it was unbelievable that he would forget to complete his directions in this way. He continued on past the heaps of building materials and furniture and went into a very broad corridor off which the doors of some large wards opened; within, there were beds in a row, occupied by patients, and also some mattresses set up in the aisle between the beds, with patients on them. They must be the patients from the other pavilions placed there while the bricklayers were fixing theirs up. At the end of the corridor was a guard, standing before a closed door. Upon seeing him approach, the guard smiled and motioned with his hands that he should hasten and said to him, "They've been waiting for you a long time. Hurry up, Mr. Suárez."

And he opened the door without announcing him. It gave access to a vestibule with many plants and armchairs, and in the middle was a table with an immense aquarium full of colored fish and aquatic grasses. It was a cool place, extremely pleasant. That's the way Cireneo Suárez experienced it, with his whole body. And even his soul was comforted. Through a high window of sky-blue glass which covered nearly the whole width of the wall, a torrent of polished light was penetrating. He looked about and from a doorway a nurse, all in white, even her shoes and cap, motioned to him to come in, smiling at him affectionately as if she were acquainted with him and liked him. He observed her and did not recall having seen her, since she was not the one who had remained in the doorway of his supervisor's room when the doctor and the intern were circling around him pronouncing enigmatic words.

"Ward number four. Mr. Teodoro Benegas. I am coming to see him," exclaimed Cireneo Suárez, who still retained his green card in the tips of his fingers.

"Come in, Mr. Suárez. He's this way. Do you want to leave your coat?"

"I'm not hot, thank you. I'd like to get there. I've been going in circles around the hospital for more than half an hour."

Suárez experienced some annoyance in the face of this unusual invitation to remove his coat, for he recalled that his shirt was not very clean, and he thought he noticed an attempt to humiliate him in the nurse's suggestion. For that reason he had explained what they had not asked him. More than one courtesy regarding his comfort seemed to him a purposeful allusion. In the next little room, which was visible through the door which the nurse opened, an elderly couple was waiting, in an obvious state of agitation, along with a woman, possibly their daughter, her hair already gray.

"The fact is, they're waiting for you, Mr. Suárez," added the nurse with exaggerated kindness.

"All this can be counter-productive," said the old man with a reproachful tone, addressing his wife but in a voice loud enough for the rest to hear.

"We've come from San Luis, and today is the twelfth, the last day of the period," answered the old woman looking at Suárez with maternal entreaty, while the daughter brought her diminutive handkerchief to her mouth. She said nothing, but she directed a glance at Suárez more severe than the words of her parents. Cireneo was confused and felt a kind of regret for having come to the hospital after having promised himself not to set foot there again. He answered their gaze with another severe look and allowed the nurse to take the green card from his hand.

"*Cer*eneo or *Cir*eneo?" she asked, looking it over glancingly.

"Whatever it says there," he answered, still without knowing what to hold onto with respect to that inquisitiveness. It was stupid. He had neither the desire nor the need, much less the obligation, to visit his supervisor, with whom he had fulfilled his duty and then some the afternoon before. At this moment he was quite certain he had been dealing with a charlatan—just as the man had seemed in the Company ever since joining it—and that his illness was a pretext for being absent for who knows how long from his office, surrounded by comforts and hospitality. He didn't understand how he could have said to him, on leaving, "You know that I am completely at your service in any way you might need me, and that you can ask me for anything in which I might help you." It was a formula, but he ought not to have used it. Then his supervisor responded—he remembered it as if hearing it now—: "You don't owe me anything here. Your obligations end at my office door." "Oh, no, sir! I must serve you everywhere, not merely at the office. And here more than ever, since you are ill." He had said this, he didn't know why, and he regretted it at once. Immediately his supervisor touched the button of an electric bell and then it was that the doctor, the intern, and the nurse had appeared. After a few moments had passed, his supervisor went on as if he hadn't yet taken in Cireneo's words—he called him "*Cer*eneo," hence the mixups—: "Oh! In everything? Remember that you said it spontaneously, on your own hook," he exclaimed, rubbing his hands, and he was about to finish that joyful ratification when the doctor, the intern, and the nurse entered. For they must have been waiting for the agreed-upon signal in the adjoining room. Now he was certain that the clerk who had given him the card was that very nurse, and that the one before him now was the one who had been attending to his supervisor.

"I've come to see Mr. Teodoro Benegas, ma'am."

"Mr. Teodoro Benegas?" asked the old man, surprised. "What does this fellow mean?"

"He must be trying to excuse his being so late," answered the daughter in a tone of voice that Cireneo would never have supposed would correspond to her face. A sweet voice, that of a child, which left a fragrant caress in the ambience of the little room.

"I wonder if he's not just like the others, like back in nineteen thirty-six. Remember?"

"I was just thinking about that, too," the old woman replied. "The same way of just coming in late, acting absentminded, pretending he doesn't know what's going on."

A door opened, and with his head a doctor invited him to enter. He had his rubber gloves on and the antiseptic mask.

"Ward number four," Cireneo succeeded in saying as he crossed the threshold.

This room was smaller and nearly dark. He, at least, could see very little.

"They are waiting for you."

"Who? My supervisor?"

"Your supervisor, the examining board, and your humble servant. I thought you might stay away too, like the friend that you are. Reprobate! Determined to make me come a cropper! But let's not delay, Mr. Suárez. I ought to warn you that you will see a lot of people, more than you've seen on similar occasions. Don't be frightened, and try to keep calm. I'll do likewise, although today is not a happy day for me. The day before the thirteenth, as in all my campaigns. Talk about the evil eye! Did you meet my fiancée in the waiting room? Every year she comes with her parents to witness the examinations, and that is what makes me the most nervous. As if they could help me by doing that! The other way around!"

"Those people out there?"

"Don't say 'those people.' They might be able to hear you. They are my future parents-in-law. He is an important politician in San Luis, the uncle of General Quijada. Compulsively, he has undertaken to use his influence, and that has been prejudicial to me. There isn't any influence worth anything around here," he went on while he smoothly removed Cireneo's coat, untied his tie, and took off his collar with obliging care. "I mean, among the candidates. But I am the sort that as soon as I find out they want to give me a hand, I fall apart. Undress now."

"Every minute that goes by is counted, from the moment the patient enters," said a man with white hair through the crack in the door. He too was wearing a smock and the other adornments of a doctor.

"Get undressed?"

"Oh, no. Only your shirt. And if for any reason you should wish to remove your undershirt, since you haven't come properly prepared, you may do so. But hurry, I beg of you, as the time is running now on my clock, since you came into the vestibule. It used to be a double clock, for timing chess matches."

Cireneo became indignant, without showing it, as he usually did when something happened that was superior to his capacity for resistance. Suddenly a light went on in his mind. Perhaps they had taken him literally, with his promise before the witnesses, and must be going to have him keep his word to serve his supervisor in every way. They must be going to extract blood for a transfusion. Nothing else occurred to him. *I must serve you everywhere, not merely in the office.*

"Transfusion?"

"We'll see later on. Hurry, please."

And the doctor, that is, the one who had received him and practically disrobed him, disappeared through the door which, on being opened, allowed a blast of disinfectant odor to enter. He saw an operating table and numerous physicians, all in white smocks, standing about. He entered perplexed. He hung his jacket and his shirt on the clothes rack, and put his collar and tie on top.

"Can't you tell me what you're going to do?"

That question provoked general laughter. Even the old doctor who had warned that time was being charged to the candidate seemed quite amused at the idea. It was an operating room, with a large, wide window, and much bigger than he had thought upon entering. There were numerous rows of seats behind the seats for the panel of judges, and all of them occupied, possibly by students. In the center was only the operating table, and a small stand surrounded by surgeon's instruments, bottles of gas, flasks, and scissors.

On the wall hung a small, square sign, with a dark frame. It said:

NO SMOKING
CIGARS AND PIPES

The second line had been added later, evidently.

A nurse approached him and began to cut his hair, precisely where he had that cyst—or fibroma, as his supervisor called it. Then his bewildered brain lit up again because, in truth, without telling him so, they had examined him yesterday, and on the form was recorded the origin and progress of that protuberance. Twenty years before, when he was twelve or thirteen and still going to school, he had stopped before the entrance of a circus where clowns, trained animals and trapeze artists were performing. There were large colored posters showing lions and their tamer, with letters in the shape of branches. From behind, a school companion had brutally thrown a rock which struck him on the crown. He hadn't bled. A bump formed which disappeared with time, and ten years later, slowly, a diminutive little ball began forming—like a sugar almond—which little by little enlarged its volume: a shot, a pea, a hazel nut, a walnut.

That was all that had happened then, twenty years ago. And if it weren't for the fact that his supervisor insisted on his getting examined, and in the end he had managed it on that afternoon of the visit, Cireneo would have died an old man with his wen. That's what he had called it, in keeping with the ordinary, familiar nomenclature, until he heard them speak of fibromas and cysts. Now his ailment had become complicated; but how was it possible that they would operate on him without warning him of anything, without consulting him, without letting his relatives know, without his changing clothes? All this was simply an abuse.

"Unless it's a question of something very serious that they might have wanted to hide from me," he thought.

What grieved him most was the condition of his underwear. As far as their methods went, the way in which they had taken him by surprise, closing in around him without defense, all this seemed an outrage, a violation of principles. But he didn't say anything that might compromise his already sufficiently unhappy situation.

"I am not prepared," he exclaimed, after having stood a few moments facing the audience, arms crossed over his undershirt, which was in fact the worst one he had. He was determined to resist, although he had a vague suspicion that he would not be able to carry it beyond certain limits. He had not forgotten that this institute was a dependency of the State. He added:

"I beg you, I implore your excellencies the physicians to grant me an extension of time."

Meanwhile the nurse had completed her task and was now running a dry razor, biting in as it was shaving him, over the spot she had cleared.

"After the diagnosis has been made, you wouldn't want to wait now until the fibroma or whatever it is we are looking at may have perforated the base of the cranium."

"Of course not, gentlemen," replied Cireneo. "I am only requesting that you allow me to present myself properly."

The whole audience laughed again and exchanged unintelligible words among themselves. The nurse finished her job and withdrew.

"Has the Recording Secretary been called?"

"In due time, the time on your clock, Mr. Cáceres. The hour-and-a-half has been reduced to an hour and ten minutes."

"I asked about the Recording Secretary and not the clock nor the time, Professor. It seems to me that in order to begin deducting the time from me it is necessary for the Recording Secretary to be present here, as the regulation provides."

"The Recording Secretary is here, waiting for you, Mr. Cáceres," a gentleman said from a corner; he too was dressed in a white smock, with sleeves of lamé over those of the smock, sitting before a small table with an enormous open book and a pen holder in his hand. He was turning the pages, slipping them with his index finger as if he wished to make sure that none had been left blank, and he was looking over his eyeglasses at Cireneo.

The light which was coming in through the wide window was diminishing rapidly, and it was getting cooler. Cireneo felt it on his bare arms and on the recently shaved part of his head.

"The natural illumination is coming to an end, the artificial surgical lamp is coming on, with the temperature having decreased to 52 degrees. You may verify it with the thermometer, if you wish," explained the Recording Secretary.

"This is an utter humiliation for me," said Cireneo Suárez, still in the same spot, very depressed, without enough strength to protest or the desire to lay himself down on the operating table. Four nurses, two on each side, drew near him. Smoothly they took hold of separate parts of his body and made him bend over. Two of them passed their arms around his abdomen, the other two around his legs. When he was spread over, they took a few steps backward and bore him lengthwise over the operating table and left him stretched out face down upon it without Cireneo managing to resist or say a word. It had all been one really admirable, combined movement. Immediately, with extraordinary rapidity and in contrast to the gentleness of their earlier maneuvers, they fastened him down solidly. With white straps fixed to the table, they tied his feet by the ankles, his legs at the thigh, his waist, his wrists, his arms at the elbows, his neck. They passed the straps through the buckles and locked them down. He remained unable to move, literally glued to the operating table. Cireneo was sweating from anger, shame, amazement, impotence. One of the nurses removed his shoes quickly. Another threw a white sheet over his body, still another placed a pillow beneath his cheek. Since the strap was so tight over his neck, he felt they were strangling him. But the nurse soon noticed it and adjusted the strap and the pillow until all discomfort disappeared as if he himself had done it.

"Let's see how you're doing," the intern said into his ear as he was examining him, the same one Cireneo had taken for a doctor. But he was simply a student of long standing whom they had held back in Surgery eleven times in eight years, defeats which had left him completely disheartened.

"I have obligations at the Company, too," answered Cireneo as a way of responding. "I have my responsibilities." He was thinking that at a quarter to twelve his absence without giving previous notice would be taken heed of, and this being the third occurrence of the month they could suspend him with no excuse to avail him, and especially that of an operation, which he should have been able to warn them about beforehand. His supervisor, would he help him now, after the dirty trick he had just played?

"This is your twelfth examination in surgery, Mr. Cáceres, and your final opportunity. I must warn you, in conformance with the statute, " the Recording Secretary announced in a cold voice, "the eleven previous failures which are recorded on their respective folios are considered as known and accepted. In like manner I must warn the candidate, Mr. Gregorio Cáceres, that a new postponement will mean definitive failure and the loss of any new opportunity until ten years have passed. But, since your age by then will exceed the allowable limits even including all tolerances, exceptions, and favors that may be granted, the candidate, Mr. Gregorio Cáceres, would have no appeal except to the High Council of Academic Instance, with the testimony of sponsors, a situation governed by the standards of the lecture hall."

The hall heard that sentence by the Recording Secretary in religious silence.

"I know that already," Cáceres answered drily. "I have heard that lecture on regulations eleven times before, and now with this, it makes twelve."

In reality he was frightened and therefore he used all his energy in his reply. He did not want the onlookers, the professors, and his fellow students to perceive the slightest upset or nervousness in his voice.

"First: diagnosis," one of the doctors in the first row to the left broke in. "Disjunctives in the diagnosis are unacceptable."

"It is simple," Cáceres replied immediately. "Fibroma of the scalp."

"Give all possible alternatives, the only admissible one, and its conditions."

Cáceres palpated the protuberance again.

"Cancer."

"Note that down, Mr. Recording Secretary," the President of the examining board ordered with a magisterial voice.

"One moment, please," the Recording Secretary said hastily, and he began to write rapidly at the same time as he was reading out in a clear voice, "In Buenos Aires, capital of the Republic of Argentina, at ten thirty-eight A.M. on this twelfth day of December—"

"That should have been done already, Mr. Secretary," Cáceres rebuked him while with his elbow he stopped the clock placed at the head of the operating table.

"Allow me, Mr. Cáceres. The new municipal decree of the sixth of the current month prohibits the use of printed forms and requires the complete text of the examination document be written during the examination itself. Nurse, please do not permit the clock to be interrupted again."

"Let the candidate who is offering Injections pass first," another of the physicians recommended with a powerful voice.

"Isn't that also in Mr. Cáceres's examination?" the Recording Secretary interrupted.

"No, of course not," the elderly President of the examining board replied. "We are also making use of this session to examine Mr. Arturo Cuelles, a first-year assistant postponed because of a failing mark."

"Here!" broke out a young man with an incipient mustache.

Cáceres took himself to one side, and the candidate Cuelles approached the operating table. The professors had raised the seats of their swivel chairs, and now they were sitting at a height above the operating table. They had a perfectly good command of the scene.

"He has two ampoules; there are no more," warned the head intern in charge of equipment, who was entrusted with supplying the instruments, syringes, and ampoules.

"Place the injections so that the anesthetic will last for two hours, or at least two hours and a half," the President explained. "Six insertions, placed without affecting the ganglia. Incomplete anesthesia of any of the points within the operating field is inadmissible. A single error with any of the six insertions, computed at four points each, twenty-four in all, means a postponement, and that would be your second, Mr. Cuello."

"Cuelles."

"Mr. Cuelles."

"Excuse me " exclaimed the Recording Secretary. "I will have to bring the other book for this examination; it was completely unforeseen. I assumed that Mr. Cáceres would have the anesthesia in his care."

"You assumed wrong, Mr. Ordóñez. It is a question of two examinations, as you were advised in the memo from the secretariat."

"Yes, yes, I don't argue that, Mr. Professor President. I only said I was going to search for the other book, for it is already prepared, or it ought to be."

"You said 'unforeseen,'" added young Cuelles. "Look at the program for today before you speak."

"I beg all your pardons, a thousand times. But let your excellencies the examiners consider that today, at this very hour, two hundred boards are functioning in this very pavilion, and that I have already attended six examinations; two passes and four failures."

Cuelles was examining the syringe while supporting in his left hand the ampoule which the head intern in charge of equipment had just handed him.

"A single error, without taking into account the topography of the affected zone? I assume that your excellencies the examiners will have taken into consideration the zone, the characteristics of the skin, the state of nervousness of the patient, and the quality of novocaine which is made in this country. Two ampoules is an unjustifiable limitation. I want the Recording Secretary to note down my observation."

"When he returns. Begin your examination."

Meanwhile, Cáceres was walking up and down beside the operating table. When he managed to draw close to Cireneo's ear, he did not cease to implore him: "Don't make me look bad, I beg you, in the name of what you love most in all the world."

"Your excellencies the professors will note that this is a question of a doliocephalic cranium, asymmetrical, with a thick coriaceous dermis. If I have the option to challenge this patient, I do so. Or to request a new date, or a different time. In case the answer is negative, I request, to be recorded in the minutes—" the Secretary returned at that moment, which provoked attention—" a third ampoule, always within the limit of six insertions, but at least one of them ganglional. As for the six insertions with two ampoules, that is an absurd margin, above all considering the quality of the candidate in surgery, with eleven postponements. It is an absurd margin. My argument is supported by the unrescinded statute of the year one thousand nine hundred thirty-nine, which looks out for the patient by extending the margin of anesthesia by one third over that fixed by the tribunal. I am within my right, Mr. President?"

"No, Mr. Cuelles. That statute refers to fractures and laparotomies. It actually excludes cutaneous surgery and, more exactly, the scalp."

"That is correct, Mr. President," assented the Recording Secretary. "The regulation which Mr. Cuelles cites is not of that sort, but an ordinance for the protection of patients in which minimal conditions of analgesia have occurred because of technical errors of insertion. It does not speak to the quality of the medicine."

"Then," answered Cuelles, turning over the syringe and the already opened ampoule to the head assistant, "I must point out that the curriculum only speaks of one error, without qualification, it being understood that such an error occurs if it causes the anesthesia of an adjacent zone and leaves feeling in the operating area. I will only accept with this proviso: an error will not be counted if the adjacent zone goes to sleep through a peculiar complex of tissues. Puigwehr's phenomenon. I have that right."

"Granted," said the President. "Granted the use of three ampoules with six insertions, with Mr. Cáceres, the candidate in Surgery, authorized to indicate at his own discretion the distribution of the shots according to the incision, its area and depth, and the time for the surgery and the suturing."

"Agreed," Cuelles said, taking back the syringe and the ampoule out of the intern's hands.

"Agreed," assented Cáceres. "Major injection, oblique, crosswise: north-south."

And approaching his fellow student, he advised him, "Don't take it into your head to go in for the rachidian bulb if you don't have a diploma, I ask you, for God's sake. You're going to start to lose points, and this is crucial for your average. Do the insertions to conform with article 9, section C."

Cireneo was bewildered, and he was ready either to weep or to curse. He perceived a vague, disagreeable odor and made an effort to discover what it was; his face became heated as if from a wave of blood. The strap around his neck clung to him. One leg was beginning to cramp. He felt the nurse putting his shoes back on him.

"If you could only open the window ... I'm so hot," he mumbled.

"Impossible. Be still," said the professor in front of him, patting him on the arm. The hall was sinking into a gradually deeper shadow.

The preparatory part was completed. Doctors and students plunged their hands into their pockets and pulled out money, passing it around from hand to hand.

"Fifty to thirty. As usual, Dr. Campisto."

"Okay. Give it to the nurse."

"Carmela, take it, you're the banker. A hundred and seventy pesos. Do you want any more?"

"No, Doctor. Let's wait."

"They're betting!" thought Cireneo.

"I'll see that. And I'll double you, Doctor," said Cáceres, mortified.

The Recording Secretary was writing rapidly. But he had time to take out his wallet and hand over ten pesos to a nurse who apparently was busy picking up the bets, placing the money between her fingers and noting some figures down on a piece of paper.

"It's going three to one, against. Bets also taken, changing the odds throughout the operation, up to the full incision."

Cuelles began to push the injection needle in. He was hesitantly sounding out the situation, and only after several tests did he decide to inject the anesthetic.

"Doliocephalic, and with the hide of a zebu."

"It will be necessary to set up a neon lamp. You can scarcely see."

"That is within your right, Mr. Cáceres."

"What kind of lamp?"

"Oblong, two hundred fifty candlepower, seventy-five centimeters above."

"Of course. Nurse, you heard it now. Mr. Secretary, note down the candidate's choice in the minutes."

"My opinion is that we should put down this detail as unfavorable for the examination, that is, two points negative. With that lamp you can't see anything; instead, it will interfere with the diffused overhead light because of its placement, shape, and height."

"I said, oblong, two hundred fifty candlepower, seventy-five centimeters above," Cáceres repeated, indignant.

"Ah! I withdraw my observation, and beg your pardon."

Cuelles continued stabbing with the needle. For the sixth time.

"The last one. May I withdraw now?"

"Of course, Mr. Cuelles. They will tell you the results of the examination in the office once the effectiveness is confirmed."

The students, who had filled the benches of the hall, broke out into applause. There was no doubt they stayed sympathetic to him as they considered the different turns undergone by his examination, his preliminary declaration, which was felt as an indispensable proof of his mastery of the subject, and perhaps the reliability of his injections. On going out, Cuelles slapped Cáceres on the shoulder.

"It looks to me that with that thick skull you're going to flunk out again, friend."

Cireneo didn't understand very well what all those phrases meant, though he was trying not to lose the thread of everything that was done and said. The first prick hurt him until the needle had penetrated deeply. In his bones he heard the liquid spilling beneath his skin. The other pricks hurt him less.

"Can't someone let the Company know?" he asked into the air. "To say I'm not feeling well? I'm getting upset."

"Don't talk baloney, now," Cáceres told him. And approaching his ear, "Don't do that, I beg you. Try to be calm. You already see there is a conspiracy against my future father-in-law, and they're taking bets at three to one; that's enough to discourage anybody."

"Conspiracy?" exclaimed Cireneo in surprise, and he tried uselessly to raise his head.

"You heard it," Cáceres continued into his ear. "A political situation. This examining board belongs to the opposition, and they've made up their minds to bring me down."

The Recording Secretary exclaimed in a solemn voice:

"Diagnosis: fibroma. Variant of likely choice, one: cancer. You may begin when you wish, Mr. Cáceres. It is ten fifty-six. Record that."

"The time required for bringing the lamp has to be deducted. Stop the clock, nurse."

"Granted," the President of the examining board ratified the request, and the nurse pressed the spring to interrupt the running of the clock.

"We're almost in the dark."

"Naturally. Until they bring the lamp. You know perfectly well that one cannot do a surgical examination with natural light alone, exposed to alterations that could be disastrous. Don't be in such a hurry, we'll see how you do later on."

"It's clouded over suddenly," Cireneo insisted. "Nurse, can't they phone the Company that I'm here?"

"Don't get disturbed, please. Be calm," the nurse answered him, caressing his hand softly.

"It was a magnificent day," Cireneo went on, because speaking soothed him.

"Don't talk, your head will become congested unnecessarily."

It seemed to Cireneo that his head was of a monstrous size. It had become swollen and turned to stone. That's what it felt like to him: enormous and tight. Words, the sounds of the instruments in the flasks, he was hearing these clearly. He even heard the blows of the carpenters' hammers driving nails in far-off wings of the hospital. His own voice resonated in his cranium as if between cement walls, but his sense of hearing perceived it without deformation.

"Seventy-two, seventy-three, seventy-four," the Recording Secretary was counting, amusing himself by noting the hammer blows, as if it were customary in his position.

Cireneo felt that his blood was thrusting at the pulses in his wrists and likewise that it was throbbing, silently, in the region where he had been anesthetized. Sometimes the beating and the pulsations coincided with the remote hammer blows. He also felt in his head that they were striking it gently with rubber hammers. It seemed to him that the Recording Secretary counted every two pulsations as one and that it was the carpenter who was beating the time of the count with his hammer. He amused himself for a few seconds supervising the Secretary's bookkeeping; he was doing all right ... ninety-eight, ninety-nine.... Suddenly the noise stopped, and the hammering of his blood was as though it were breaking out into a gallop.

Cáceres was palpating the fibroma carefully; he took it delicately on the balls of his fingers and tried to pull it up to verify if it was deeply rooted or not.

"This is connected to the thalamus, I'm thinking. I hope it won't be necessary to trepan...."

The electrician came, dressed in a white smock and rubber insulating gloves like they usually wear, white ones, and duly set up the lamp at seventy-five centimeters, angled to the north-northeast, with a 250 candlepower bulb, which the Recording Secretary had him turn on. The lamp threw a warmth over Cireneo's head which he felt on the back of his neck and on the part of his ear covered by the cloth. He also felt warmth and a bluish light beneath the sheet that covered him.

"This lamp is not the one I asked for; it's not oblong, it's periform."

"Those are the ones that are used now, Mr. Student," answered the electrician.

"It already was apparent to me that Mr. Cáceres was committing an error when he indicated the shape of the bulb, since for three months now they have made only periform bulbs for this type of illumination. But as he insisted, I kept quiet."

"If you will permit me, Mr. President, rather than keeping quiet, you consented. Here it is affirmed: 'Ah, I withdraw my observation and beg your pardon.' But there is also the wink recorded here with which you accompanied the words that doubtless referred to Mr. Cáceres' persistence in the error."

"Of course, of course. I wanted the facts to demonstrate Mr. Cáceres' obstinacy in this error."

"It is not an error, given the fact that the oblong bulb is classic. If they are not being made now, that is not my fault. And the periform, which officially supplants the earlier shape, should be understood for the classic form, as I said."

"Enough," interrupted the President of the Board. "You have to go on, or rather begin, with your examination. There are three hundred seventh-year surgery students, Group B, several times postponed, who are waiting. Mr. Cáceres must accept two negative points."

"Approved," the other members of the board confirmed.

"By no means, your excellencies the President and other members of the board; by no means," Cáceres exclaimed. "I am not here to stake my career, that is, my life, on little matters. I accept the lamp, but I reserve the right of appeal at the first opportunity for a hearing. The condition is, Mr. Recording Secretary, that for that occasion I will have the lamp checked by an expert electro-technician, and that I will request official reports concerning the change in the illuminating system, about which no information has been passed on to us in writing."

"Agreed," the President pronounced sentence.

An enormous and scorching silence was produced, as if a discharge of infrared waves were invading the operating room.

"Pay attention to the signal to begin," the President went on. "One, two, three."

"Longitudinal incision," and Cáceres was demonstrating his surgeon's hand.

Cireneo clearly felt the cold scalpel that was cutting his scalp with nimble zeal, a painless incision, but with a sensation which was tactile.

"Just like saddler's leather," Cáceres commented, wrestling to complete the cut. "Straight as a rule. Do the jurors wish to verify it?"

"Continue."

Cáceres leaned down until his lips were touching the outer ear outside the sheet. Cireneo felt the warmth of his breath.

"Don't scream, I beg you in the name of whatever you love most. That gets negative points. This is the only thing I ask you."

"Hurry up, headbone," answered the patient, who was sweating in torrents beneath the sheet, from head to feet. Never in all his life had he ever said a word backwards, but at this moment he held back from pronouncing the pejorative "bonehead" which he had wanted to use, and with all naturalness he said it the other way. He had tried it out when he saw the intern with the little moustache before they had put him in his shroud—that was how he thought of it—and, now having learned it, he let it out. "Bonehead," he thought: a word that he had never pronounced in the normal way either. He didn't know what it meant, except that it was an insult. He kept thinking of it while the scalpel pursued its bloody task.

"Headbone? You want me to go under," Cáceres said out loud, and continued working with difficulty because of the resistance of the skin. He was panting. The head intern helped him by reaching various instruments for him.

"You're talking gibberish; use the #3 back-bent scissors," he suggested to Cáceres. The latter didn't reply nor pay any attention. He was blinded, in effect. And that was an assistance that represented five points for him. The members of the board didn't notice, or they pretended not to. They went on handing money back and forth, and also with those in the galleries, but without saying anything. Finger signals sufficed, which now signified four to one, or three and a half, with the gesture of cutting one of the fingers with the other hand.

"This scalpel is like a toy sword. It won't cut as well as a cobbler's *furchetta*," he protested. "Let the Recording Secretary note this protest."

"It's possible the nurses have made a mistake."

"Bring him the set of sealed scalpels."

"Those were also sealed."

"There was no such error, if your excellencies the doctors will pardon me," replied the nurse who was watching the clock and who had taken Cireneo's hand, which she was toying with, caressing it with an amorous touch. "I sterilized the three that were on top of the cupboard in the office."

"And who ordered you to choose those three, precisely those three?"

"Me?"

"Sabotage!" screamed Cáceres indignantly and threw the scalpel to the floor.

Cireneo felt that a warm wave was flooding over his face. But this time it was really blood, not shame. "A vein," he thought, while the blood that was falling down his cheek slipped toward his mouth. He tasted it. It was blood, in fact. His blood. The head intern was mopping at the hemorrhage, cleaning the patient's face without looking and thrusting one hand with a gauze pad underneath the cloth that covered him, so that he sometimes drew the gauze through his mouth as well as over his eyes and ear.

"*Ciocolatto*," he said into his ear, slowly. And to Cáceres, "Here are some other scalpels. Don't protest over nothing. You'll get yourself into a tangle. Especially with the panel, for you have to put up with this pachyderm."

"Continue operating with number two," said the President of the board. "Discard the other one." A nurse had already gathered it up, depositing it in the sink.

"It's a pleasure this way," continued Cáceres, who was cutting now with greater ease.

Cireneo felt no pain from the cuts, but he did have the sensation as if they might be disconnecting a hat that was stuck tightly to his head.

When Cuelles had left, he had shut the door without putting on the latch. Pushing it open softly, a scrawny cat penetrated the room, slowly and gracefully, but with a repulsive appearance. It looked a filthy green, or as if badly washed. Like certain people, it had an extremely undistinguished appearance together with an arrogant bearing. It rubbed its body from head to tail against a nurse's leg. She shoved it away, pushing at it delicately with her foot. The cat meowed piteously, looking toward the operating table with an imploring attitude. Cireneo shivered.

"Take the cat out," the Recording Secretary ordered.

"It's not my job," the nurse answered. "That's from getting them into bad habits."

One of the spectators got up, took the cat out, and shut the door, carefully latching it. All in silence, solemnly.

No one remarked on the scene because others of the sort or close to it were always happening whenever someone out of carelessness went through the door without shutting it well. Besides, there were surgeons who took pleasure in working surrounded by cats. They were just able to do it.

The Recording Secretary meanwhile was pursuing the count of hammer-blows which had resumed a short while ago, with the same rhythm as before: two hundred and six, two hundred and seven....

"At this point in the examination, I am ratifying the diagnosis: lipofibroma, that is in its generic form, a fibroma, as it should already be recorded in the minutes."

"You are just beginning. You still haven't even begun to separate the scalp, or are you aware of that, Mr. Cáceres?"

"Aware of it?"

"On the other hand, that is the diagnosis already marked down on his record form. It is Dr. Andreu's, not yours."

"I have never seen such a form. I accompanied Dr. Andreu, I have talked with him, but I have not seen the record, and I am not discussing that record now, absolutely not; it cannot be of any influence upon the diagnosis, whether it is exact or erroneous." Cáceres was certain that it was exact. "I assumed the responsibility and I am maintaining it honorably, totally."

He went on operating while he was speaking. The voice of the chief of the maintenance men was heard: nine hundred twenty-six, nine hundred twenty-seven....

"I'm falling apart, Doctor," Cireneo exclaimed with the voice of a death rattle. "Let me get up. I'm going to pieces." This last he said with self-assurance and firmness.

"You're out of your head, a little crazy," the nurse said. "What kind of pieces do you mean?"

"I'm going to faint. My strength is gone."

"It's the effect of the injection. What else?"

"Just a general coming from together. My whole body, nurse. It would be shameful for me. Tell the doctor to let me go, and I promise him I will return right away. I need air, and to go to the men's room."

"A major coming-from-together? Or a minor one? Say it in one word."

"My heart is going to quit, Doctor. It's worse than dying."

"I wonder if you really know what that is!"

"The depressed state of the patient is not an unnegligible factor in these circumstances," the President suggested. He was satisfied with the course of the examination, having made bets up to five to one.

"I beg the examining board to avoid situations that might contribute to the weakening of my spirit, which is already sufficiently distressed."

After fifty minutes of Cáceres' being engaged in slicing cleanly away at the fibroma in order to remove it, the Recording Secretary warned: "An hour and a half, exactly."

"The first period, on the dot," added one of the panelists.

"There is a choice here. Shall the examining board adjourn and remove itself to a nearby room for fifteen minutes, or shall we go on with the second period?" explained the Recording Secretary. "It's time for the break."

"Do you prefer to forego the interruption and continue, Mr. Cáceres? Your patient is in a hopeless moral state, and it would not be surprising if we didn't need the nurses to clean him up."

"No, I prefer to rest. I am exhausted."

Cáceres deposited his scalpel in the flask.

"Let's take a rest," the students said in a chorus.

"First, I must warn you of the possibility that the effects of the anesthesia might wear off before the end of his operation. One of the injections was released into the fatty tissue."

"That's another matter. But that is still the responsibility of the one who was being examined earlier."

"I know that. I want to let you know that to break now could have an influence on whether you might have to proceed with the operation as is, without additional anesthesia."

"You know, of course, that moaning or screaming by the patient will be detrimental to your total number of points."

"Everything considered, I shall opt for the break. My pulse is wavering; I am wilted. I don't have the strength in me to go on, your excellencies the judges and staff."

Those in the galleries, together with the attending physicians, began to withdraw. Cáceres went out clasped in the arms of the head intern who was encouraging him with little pats on the shoulder, repeating several times, "The suture on that vein was fantastic, just fantastic—not even Dr. Erissi could have done it."

Cireneo and the nurse remained alone. The hammering had ceased, as well as all other sounds from outside. With a fan the nurse was creating a breeze beneath the sheet.

"Take the sheet off me, nurse, and the straps too. I need to get up. Really, I am about to go to pieces."

He felt someone removing his shoes. It was another nurse, assigned to help him at the suggestion of the person in charge of staffing.

"Now you will rest a little better. We'll open a window so the fresh air can come in and ventilate this place. You aren't as hygienic as we would like to have you, Mr. Suárez."

"You must be a single man," added the head nurse. "If you're about to lose control of yourself, do you want me to call the clean-up nurse? He will be able to remove your clothing and facilitate your evacuations, major and minor. Don't be ashamed in front of us. We are accustomed to it. We've seen much worse sights, I can tell you. Besides, it's our business."

"Has he taken out the whole fibroma?" the other nurse asked.

"Be still now, don't try to get loose. It's useless, you'll aggravate your discomfort if you get your neck muscles tense. Just wait a little."

"But, the fibroma ... is it gone?"

"No. You can look, if you like."

The nurse drew near. She was carrying Cireneo's shoes in her hand, dangling by the laces.

"That's right. There's a lot left. It looks like a hen's egg before it was laid. See how round it is, and with its little veins?"

"Get away, now, Clotilde. Let's not have a case of infection. Leave us awhile so that Mr. Suárez can rest. He is sweating." And beneath the sheet she was wiping off his perspiration, softly and lovingly.

"I'll just use the time then to polish his shoes."

And she went out.

The nurse who had been attending to him took him by the hand once more, with real tenderness.

"Mr. Suárez.... Have you suffered a great deal? You can't imagine how much sympathy I feel for you. You're not in good hands, I can tell you."

"It's unbelievable, isn't it, nurse?" And with energy in his voice: "It's an outrage!"

"Don't shout! And you know why I tell you that. All constitutional guarantees have been suspended."

"I know, I know it," Cireneo admitted, lowering his voice.

"Why did you get a green card, for an operation?" and she pressed his hand. "I have suffered as much as you have, or more, ever since you came in. I think Cáceres will be flunked."

"Why don't you let me loose, nurse? That is, if you are fond of me, as you say."

"Are you thinking of escaping, in your condition?"

"Why did you ask me that about the green card?"

"There are other cards: yellow, white, pink. It's examination time now, and everyone is angling for patients. There are some employees at the entrance desk that collect fifty pesos a patient. Afterward they argue about divvying up."

"And why do you think they are going to give Dr. Cáceres another postponement?" Cireneo asked as if it were rather important to him.

"The worst is yet to come! One can see right away that you're a loyal person. The real one to blame is your supervisor, I'm absolutely sure of it."

"I thought so from the first moment. He took me at my word without a second thought."

"I knew you would come today."

"Me? No one mentioned it to me."

"That wasn't necessary," and, smiling kindly, she went on, "You see, though, that you have come."

"I came to see my boss."

"That's what they all think, that they have come for other reasons. They all say the same, after they receive the order."

"What order?"

"Don't you remember that yesterday, as you were going out, a male nurse told you, 'I hope to see you around here some morning.'"

"Yes, but that wasn't addressed to me, but to someone else."

"That's what you thought. He is the one in charge of delivering 'orders.' No one ever lets him down. That's his only job. He used to be in the hypnosis section."

"How long before Mr. Cáceres will be coming back?"

"A quarter of an hour. Do you feel uncomfortable alone with me?"

"No. My upset is going away. Why?"

"They are on their break."

"Yes," said the nurse sighing. "I also suffer a great deal here. Ever since they changed the administration, things have been going badly. We nurses have to take care of the offices and fix up the rooms."

"Yes, I noticed."

"They even make us help the bricklayers at nighttime, now that they are here. A little of everything. Believe me, they are pigs! And for a hundred and fifty pesos plus meals. Tell me, haven't you noticed anything strange here since you came in?"

"Somewhat, yes. Something really out of the ordinary. Would you like me to tell you, nurse?"

"Oh, of course, that would be delightful. Up till now, no one has hit on it."

"I know it! But I don't know if anyone is listening to us." And after a pause, slowly: "This hospital is occupied."

"Of course. Go on."

"They have kidnapped the doctors, and the secret police have taken possession of the building. The whole operation is shot through with private agents."

"How did you notice that?"

"I've noticed the doorkeepers, caretakers, the gardeners and other employees surreptitiously on the watch, and also many of the nurses and even patients are watching people, observing them as if absentmindedly. I'm not stupid."

The nurse pressed his hand. "I know you're not stupid, though you are naive still. You don't know what the world is like, I'm talking about the real world."

"All the bricklayers that worked the night shift are scouts. Their jobs are fake, they just do a little work and then undo it. Do you want me to give it all to you in just a few words? This is Hell."

The nurse burst into laughter. "You are utterly mad. You're not saying anything with any common sense. Go on with your fantasies."

"Nothing comes to mind now. Take off the sheet at least so I can breathe. You can put it over me again later on."

"Be still. Don't let yourself get annoyed for no good reason. Calm yourself."

"The bricklayers are police, too."

"They want to give us a hard time because of the contracts."

"Do they work on contract, then?"

"No. Our contract."

"And that money they gave you, those that were betting? How do you know whose it is?"

"They didn't give me anything. I collected the bets but I gave the money to Carmela. You didn't see her when she came in to take off your shoes. She had her hands full of bills, between her fingers. She remembers. But she's a good girl, there's always something left for her, because when there are bets at four to one those who are betting don't always remember very well. Now I would like to ask you something, if it doesn't offend you."

Cireneo kept silent, for he was thinking about his socks, which were not any too clean.

"I would allow myself to help you, now that we are alone. Until they come back—they've got eight minutes more and a few seconds—would you let me mend your stockings? They've got several holes. That's why I put them on you again, and since...."

"Absolutely not!" Cireneo tried to cross his feet, but they were tied down and he couldn't even move them. "Apparently you're trying to humiliate me, too."

And he felt his wound throbbing as if he had his heart placed there.

"Don't be silly. Here, we are at your service, and we see everything. You are very shy. There are some male patients that just seem to be waiting for us to tell them to take off their smocks so they can be completely nude. You can see right away they want to show off. But you aren't like them, I know it. It even makes you ashamed if anyone sees your little birdie."

She took out a needle and length of thread which she had prepared and began to remove his socks so she could darn them. Cireneo did not try to move or protect himself or speak. He felt the uselessness of any attempt. Nevertheless he suggested, "I understand, I understand. It's your orders."

"Here it is obligatory to attend to our clients as if they were our own family. Another nurse is mending your shirt this very minute, and if she has time, she'll wash and iron your collar. The way you keep your underclothes is a disaster."

"I didn't know I was going to come today."

"But you always have to take precautions. It's clear that you live alone."

"Alone. Completely alone."

Never until that moment had he understood what that word meant. The nurse caressed his ankle with maternal tenderness and began her mending job. Cireneo felt that his head was continuing to grow on him, beneath the hammering of his pulse; in his ears were resounding the strokes which the Recording Secretary had counted, and a delightful dreaminess was mounting through his body.

"She has a kind hand," he thought. All of a sudden, almost, the elderly would-be parents-in-law of Cáceres came in, with their old maid daughter whose voice was that of an angel. The father drew near on tiptoe and asked him timidly, "Are you all right? How did my future son-in-law do? Are you satisfied with him? He's got a golden hand."

And in the other ear the old woman was whispering to him, "I've been praying for you this whole hour. You are our last hope. Will you hold up during this second period?"

Cireneo didn't answer and tried to control his breathing in order to distance himself from them as much as possible. They had fallen on him, defenseless and prostrate, like birds of prey ready to tear his heart out. The fiancée was whimpering with emotion and she kissed his hand.

"I ought to be kissing your feet," she exclaimed in an outburst of lyricism. "You are a hero, an angel. I had a dream that foretold the success of Gregorio Cáceres. Fifteen years we've been engaged and unable to get married because of the Faculty's intrigues—" and she broke into sobbing. "His poor parents died without having had the satisfaction of seeing him welcomed and married. It was destiny."

"They are radicals, my friend," the old man chimed in from another direction, "among the worst the country has. But they are going to come down with a big crash, believe me. This time around, I have gotten the whole Legislature, the Courts, and the Cabinet mixed up in it."

"But Antonio, it all depends on this gentleman's courage. Without him all your influence wouldn't have been worth anything at all."

"I know he'll hold up during the second period," the fiancée added with her voice that seemed born of the air. "He'll also be able to take part in our wedding joy, just as if he were family. We will always save the photograph of him in his uniform."

"Are you in the navy or in the police?" the old woman asked.

Cireneo sighed. The nurse was tickling him on the soles of his feet, meaning that he should not pay any attention to them nor contradict them. Cireneo understood.

"What should I care! I've been had!"

"He's an office boy," explained the nurse, without interrupting her task. "He works in the Juvencia Insurance Company. And he is humble and very shy."

"What's your name?" the old man asked. "I will never forget it."

The old woman passed her hand over his shoulder with maternal affection. "I love him like my own child."

The fiancée went around in front of him and taking his hand in hers, she said: "It is a terrible operation. Your skin is laid open, and the tumor is exposed to view, like a caramel egg yolk. But it's a magnificent job. Would you like to see in my little mirror?" It was an angelical question, with the clearest and most transparent of sounds coming from her divine larynx. "May I lift this sheet up a moment, nurse?"

"Don't touch that, I beg. We could have a serious mishap."

"It's been pure providence that we have come across you, Mr. Suárez. Isn't that your name?"

"Is your name Ireneo or Cireneo?" asked the old man, alarmed at the patient's muteness.

"You have his name there on the notice of examination. It's not necessary to embarrass him. He is depressed because of his situation. Besides, you can see that he is very shy. He even got into bed here completely dressed—" and again she touched him on the soles of his feet. Cireneo neither answered, nor moved, nor breathed. That signal, repeated now with a different intention, gave him the impression of some kind of joke. But the nurse kept on until he moved his foot.

"You will have to go out now, because the table is to be changed. It's not allowed to speak with the patients during an operation." She finished her sewing and accepted a five peso bill which the old man held out to her.

"All right. Courage, my son, I beg you in the name of Cireneo, your guardian saint."

"Oh yes, he will be brave, because he is valiant and he knows how to control his tongue," the fiancée affirmed with her mellifluous voice. And the three of them retired as they had entered, on tiptoe.

"They're from San Luis," said the nurse, while she was putting his socks on him. "You don't have any other problems with your underclothes? You won't feel so bad now that this business of your feet is taken care of."

"Yes," answered Cireneo with a kind of groaning sigh, so the silence would not be so oppressive, and also to prevent the nurse from coming back to the themes which were embarrassing him so, he asked, "And how is it this hospital has done so well?"

The nurse placed herself at his head and picked up his hand again. "When were you here last?"

"Yesterday."

"No, before that."

"Twenty years ago."

"Well, all right then. This place has really prospered with the new government. It's a city now. It covers twenty-two blocks, all built up."

"Do families live here also?"

"Of course. But only with recommendations. When there are three sick people in a family of five, they get installed here at government cost. On the other hand they are obligated to submit to every examination desired by the clinic students, at any time of the day or night."

"That must be annoying at night."

"There are some women that curse the day they came here because they are not left in peace for a moment, especially if they have the misfortune to suffer from any of the diseases that come up most on the examinations. They don't even have time for household chores. Sometimes they are eating when they get called. There's a system of bells and lights so they will know when they have to present themselves. They leave whatever they are doing behind, and when they get back the soup is burned or their daughters have gone off with the students."

"Don't they pay rent?"

"Very little, only for the stamps on the forms. I was a tenant when I was a child. I started my nursing career because of the Director, who had taken an interest in us. When I signed the contract I found myself absolutely enslaved for my whole life, that is, until retirement—at seventy years of age, with fifty-five years of service. Every day we went to his office, and he let us play with the patients' files, where there were photographs of nude men. Also with the flasks of pharmaceuticals, and the ones with fetuses in them. Besides, he was a dirty old man. When you're a little child you don't understand things, until at some point there's no longer any question about something being indecent."

"And why did you go to the Director's office?"

"We had fun, because he would play with us, throwing us on the floor, carrying us on his back on all fours, and playing horsey with us on his knees. He had his reasons, though at first they weren't very clear. Later on, the students used to spy on him through the corners of the windows, because we told them everything about him. Years later guards began to be set up at the corners, as you saw, and they established the secret police you mentioned. It's not true that the 'impalpable invaders,' as they are called now, occupied the buildings, but simply that that body of scouts and caretakers began to grow, enlarging itself, inserting itself everywhere, as was natural. The city—it is a city now—has been getting reformed little by little as the empty lots have disappeared and the lighting has been improved."

"Will it be long now?" Cireneo interrupted, for it seemed to him the break was being prolonged too much. His wound was beginning to give off sharp stabs of pain. "It's beginning to hurt, nurse."

"It's the anesthesia, it's barbaric how they throw it away. I would have done it better. But don't be alarmed, that little insect has a postponement for sure."

"Do you live here in the hospital, or in the city, as you call it?"

"No, I'm on contract F. I was expecting a permit, according to the steps in the schedule, but just when my dossier was waiting for the signature, the change took place."

"The change in the schedule?"

"No, the change in the administration. They removed all the directors, administrators, office managers, and bursars, in short, every one of our superiors, and installed those that are here now."

"That's what I was calling the occupation. The revolutionaries took office, jailed the administrators and office managers and replaced them with others."

"No, there wasn't any such thing. The new ones triumphed by a majority of votes among the nurses and the occupants of the houses, for they all have the right to vote, old folks as well as children. A very well-organized campaign: you should have seen it."

"But the replacing was done by sheer force, by confiscation, I'm sure of it. These things are always done that way, in the city out there, too. The same thing happened in dividing up the spoils in the municipal administration and the police. The revolutionaries removed the ones in office and set up others. To keep anybody from realizing what had happened, the new ones disguised themselves exactly like their predecessors, with mustaches, haircuts, eyebrows, or noses. They did it all like in the theatre. Those who realized the deception kept quiet because it was to their advantage. And they went on saying, "Mr. Gómez," or "Mr. Administrator," as you showed me yesterday. And it was all a lie, a great lie from foundation to roof peak."

"That did not happen here, don't talk nonsense. The chiefs might have been kidnapped as you say, but no one imitated them."

"Speak frankly. These doctors and professors are not the real ones, are they?"

The nurse pressed his hand with intense strength. "Be quiet for heaven's sake, for the love of God, I ask you. Don't say a word about such things. We would both disappear if they were to hear us. You are the devil in person."

The physicians, members of the panel, the Recording Secretary, and students all entered and placed themselves more or less in the same seats they had occupied previously.

Cáceres took the scalpel the head intern was holding out to him, and not to lose any time, the tweezers and scissors as well. The effects of the anesthesia had dissipated considerably. He was touching the fibroma insistently, and at each contact Cireneo gave a light sigh.

"It looks as though he's cutting up meat for the cat," exclaimed one of the professors who had not said a word up to that moment. "How about five to two?"

"Done."

Cireneo was experiencing very strong pain now, as if they were applying live coals to his wound, and he felt the cutting of the scalpel as a burning sensation. Doubtless they were slicing the living flesh.

"Mediocre anesthesia. Two shots lost, at least."

"Don't bother about that. We have already given a verdict in that respect. Two postponements now."

Cireneo gave a sharp scream. The pain passed completely through him, down to his feet, and he let loose a sort of howl that astonished even him.

"Stop joking around, friend," Cáceres said into his ears. "I bet they'll take off five points. And the worst is yet to come."

The rest of the operation was the torture of the inquisition. Cireneo's screams were chorused by the students. Not even the radio which they turned on at full volume, playing dance music so as not to alarm the more excitable patients, managed to blot out the howling of the wretched man. His screaming and abusive insults—at the end he lost all control whatsoever, in the broadest sense of the word—were launched in a rage, shameful in every respect, against the professors, the doctors, the authorities. He cursed his supervisor, the parents of his torturers, the spies. His shouting and epithets stood out above the waves of the loudspeaker like the comb on a cock's head. As the President of the examining board had foreseen, the electric bulb gave too little light and the sewing up of the wound had to be done gropingly. Everything was finished, and the fibroma was resting like a raw meatball in the middle of a flask. It was passed from hand to hand by the professors till it came to the Recording Secretary, who carried it out together with his books.

On being untied, Cireneo felt that his head was wobbling and that he was going to fall in a faint, like a tower shaken by an earthquake. The nurses helped him solicitously, and the

most compassionate was making a breeze around him with a
fan made of ivory and lace.

"You have to be a man and not cry. The bad moments are
over, and you must thank your lucky stars, because it really
was not a certified panel that got its hands on you. Now I can
dare to tell you, the President was not the one who really holds
that title but a substitute acting in his place, a relative who was
greedy to collect the substitute's fee."

"Leave me in peace. This has been a sacrilege." The
words choked in his throat.

"Now we'll have to change everything. You're in terrible
shape."

"I don't want to, I won't let you. You've pawed over me
enough."

Attended to in a very kindly way, he was taken to the little
waiting room where Cáceres's fiancée and future parents-in-law
had been earlier. Now it was empty, and Cireneo contemplated
the large window once more, which, it seemed to him, had
changed to a different wall.

"Your worst fears must surely have been to worry if the
Company would know anything about your tardiness," a nurse
said to him. "In this respect you may consider yourself
fortunate. Your supervisor phoned before leaving and
everything is arranged."

From another room beyond the operating room there came
the sound of voices in bitter argument.

"They must have given him a postponement?" Cireneo
asked. "He must be feeling awful."

"You have a lot to be grateful for, and that's a good thing,
Mr. Suárez. You might have had a lot worse luck. They might
have operated on your kidney or your lung, whatever they
decided. You are lucky."

"I wouldn't have allowed them to."

"It's not a question of allowing them to. They can do it, if
it is for the purpose of study, and it's however the wheel turns,
how the ball bounces. They do a diagnostic examination in
your lodgings, they get you here on some pretext, like this
business with your supervisor, and they operate on you."

"Justice would have caught up with them."

"Oh, no doubt about that, but a lot of time would have
passed. There are some lawsuits that have been going on since
the hospital was founded. When they operate on any organ
whatsoever, they always discover that you were sick."

"But they are part of the law courts, too," said the nurse
who had been taking care of Cireneo and who had been silent
until then. "There are forensic physicians and there are military

doctors, just as there are physician chaplains and homeopathic
physicians. No one knows who they are, except they
themselves. They are linked together through family
relationships and oaths among themselves, and they get their
fingers into everything. From the jails and the parish churches
they send orders to the hospital, and depending on the
assignment roster, they appoint you to service as a mounted
policeman, or they kidnap you. Didn't you notice that the man
directing traffic could be a clinician, and the surgeon a priest?
It's a question of birth. Besides, it's not a matter of professions
but of jurisdictions. As if the patients were criminals, only they
have another kind of mark, like a different sort of animal.
Oftentimes it is hidden in one's very name. It's been your good
luck that the initials of your name, C.S., have fallen your way.
That's why you requested the green card when you came in."

"I didn't ask for a green card, they gave it to me."

"Same thing. They do everything according to your
initials. Even if you had requested a visitor's card they would
have given you this one."

"And they were arguing over that?"

"Oh no! They were arguing over their bets, I told you that
already, and over how much they owe each other. Some
against the others. All those patients you saw coming in, they
have their number according to their initials. Then comes the
color, the curriculum, and the little balls with the wheel."

"But all that should be changed, I implore you."

Several physicians and staff members in white smocks
entered, arguing.

"He needs three to five votes."

"The adhesive bandage is well done. At least they'll have
to pass him on that."

"I did that bandage, Doctor, I beg your pardon," the nurse
responded.

"The worst is he had twelve bets against him."

"That has nothing to do with it; don't pay any attention."
And, whispering, "Don't argue; either they are looking for a
way to play some dirty trick on him or they have already
decided yes or no."

"Look here, it's mended now. It looks just like a surgeon's
stitches," said another nurse, whom he had not seen before and
who was holding out his shirt to him, all repaired. She spread
it out by the wings of the collar so that the dark line along the
neckband was clearly visible.

"We weren't able to wash it for you, it was too dirty and
would have taken us all afternoon."

With an enormous sense of resignation, and without saying a word, Cireneo got dressed. All of a sudden his supervisor entered, in a jubilant mood.

"Suárez, Suárez, let me shake your hand like an old and dear friend. You have saved yourself and rescued me."

"Don't make fun of me, I beg you," Cireneo answered without giving him his hand. "This has been a sacrilege."

"I didn't hear a thing, and I warn you I had my ear glued to the door in the corridor all the time. When it really hurts you can hear it as far as the street. That's why they have carpenters, radios, and strolling pill peddlers. But it's all over now, thanks be to God."

"Is he on his feet now?" asked the old woman, popping in. "Heavens, if it doesn't all seem like a dream, a farce."

"Farce, dream ..." the supervisor responded, "the important thing is that it's all been for his well-being and for my peace of mind. I couldn't bear your presence any more, Cireneo. Ten years at my office door, with that lump on your head which I've been watching grow slowly, silently, day by day. You were about to drive me crazy, and they would have thrown me out of the Company. Did you want to get ahead that way? Didn't you want to wait on the windows or go out to run down insurance? Do you know what it is to tolerate that cyst for ten years, in my doorway? I waited it out as long as I could, but I couldn't stand it any longer. Forgive me. It was a plot, actually."

"So you were only concerned about me, sir?" Cireneo responded, touched.

"Well, of course! But you didn't see it, paid no attention to it. Three times I saved you from being pensioned off. The board of directors unanimously decided to have you retired with fifteen months pay because you were a disgrace to the Company. A life insurance company, mind you!"

"You're right, sir."

Cireneo was listening as in a dream, hearing from very far off a voice that scarcely sounded like his supervisor's. His wound was giving him sharp pangs at regular intervals, as if a circular migraine were being driven from within toward the outside. He thought of his weakness, the soft spot that vanquished all his resistance, causing him to be unsuccessful in everything, great or small.

"Now you are cleansed of all that filth," his supervisor exclaimed happily, slapping him on the shoulder.

"I'm not in the mood for thinking. Let me go."

He had a cross taped over the foundation of his skull which looked rather attractive on him: one strip ran from his forehead back to his nape, another from ear to ear.

"I have taken your sins on my shoulders, and this will spare me in your eyes."

"But I've been innocent too," Cireneo said. "I don't have any resentment toward you."

"Resentment?" his boss asked with surprise and annoyance.

"I said 'resentment' as a manner of speaking. You weren't really sick, flat on your back, sir rascal?"

His supervisor let loose an insulting burst of laughter.

"That was what I had to do, and I would do it again. I'd do it a hundred times. Now, put your hat on."

Cireneo paid him no attention, didn't look at him. With his hat in his hand (since he wouldn't have been able to put it on anyway, and it was just his supervisor's joke so he could laugh at him), he went out. His boss stayed behind talking with the nurses and then plunged into the depths of the building through rooms that communicated with other *pavilions*. Cireneo heard someone calling him, with a celestial voice. He didn't turn back. He took out a cigarette. At the end of the corridor where the scaffolding and the furniture were stacked, a gust of fragrant air struck him in the face like a kiss from the blue, shining skies. It felt cool wherever he was damp, and he remembered that it was necessary for him to hurry his steps. He drew his handkerchief over his face, lit the cigarette, and continued walking as if he knew where he would come out. He didn't, of course. He encountered the caretaker, who greeted him very courteously, and afterward the invalid with the bandaged foot and crutches. All of them, the same faces exactly, for they were patrolling. Now he was deceived no longer; he knew now without any doubt that they comprised a portion of those who had been set loose in the city, peacefully taking over all the posts and dislodging the others, even the professionals. Except the inhabitants of the hospital, and the nurses, who were on contract.

At his back he heard a familiar voice calling out, "So you're leaving! You're getting away without even learning the verdict?"

Cireneo turned around in distress. It was the intern, Cáceres.

"Have you seen my fiancée and her parents around here?"

"I haven't seen anything. Leave me alone," and he continued on without knowing where he was going.

"Stop right there!" Cáceres ordered him with an imperative tone.

"Stop!" repeated the caretaker and, a moment later, the invalid. Soon there appeared the gardeners, the carpenters, and the sisters of charity.

One of the sisters said to him with an ingratiating voice, "You should stop. It's better that way," and she smiled. "Don't you want a print of Our Lord on the way to Golgotha?" She offered it to him. Cireneo looked at it, and it was exactly what he was expecting. He kept it, without offering a thank you.

"I want to get out of here," he managed to say, like a rabbit surrounded by hounds.

"Did they tell you the decision or not?" Cáceres interrogated him. "Four to one! Exactly what I predicted! But this thing is not finished yet, I swear it, Mr. Suárez."

"No? And what can we do?"

The others, attracted by Cireneo's attempt to flee, went on with their regular activities, pretending not to hear.

"You are a witness. It's a matter of sabotage, in actuality, that's what they've done to me. The rest will be taken care of by my father-in-law. I still have the option of a judicial petition, and I'm not giving it up. There's still time, until six. No matter how many times I have to lose, I'll sue the University right to the end. Come on!"

"Where to?"

"Come on, I tell you. You'll see later. We'll take a taxi."

"And your parents-in-law and your fiancée? Why aren't you going to look for them? They must be expecting you. Do they know the verdict yet?"

"Not yet. They are keeping themselves occupied until a pill they've given my fiancée's mother takes effect. It's for her heart. She has a bad heart. Come on with me right now, let's not lose any time! We have to appear before the notary public to request the petition for appeal. However, I won't go to the notary for the Hospital's Annulment Committee, but to my own private notary. We've got one hour."

He took Cireneo's arm and, in a confidential tone, explained to him: "My father-in-law is an idiot. He thinks I'll give up my struggle, and that he, for his part, will be able to do something with the pull that he has. Piss-poor pull, believe me. The radical opposition party has been out of luck for fifteen years. But he's convinced they have the same officials now as they did in 1930. Even when he's been told about them, he's never become aware of the revolutions we have had nor the invasion by the 'impalpables' and the 'ghosts,' as they are called. He's ignorant of everything. He doesn't even know anything about the submarines, believe me. For things like this, my fiancée is sharp as a tack, as you must have realized. Well, the old man is still back in 1929. And now he thinks that he'll rescue me with the help of some politicians who are dead now. But I, my friend, I rely on my own strength and I've never owed a thing to anybody. I have to protect myself even from my father-in-law. His wife, she is a good old woman, she knows all this but she pretends not to, so as not to disappoint him. That would be his death. He's suffering too, from an aneurism as big as a football. He keeps alive on garlic pills."

He dragged Cireneo violently by the arm toward another path.

"It seems you don't even know the layout here," he exclaimed. "After two in the afternoon you can't get out this way, because you'll bump into the hospital city cemetery. Come on."

"I don't understand," Cireneo said dispiritedly. "Besides, that butchery you performed on me is hurting, Cáceres."

"Let's forget that for now. This second phase is purely judicial. You don't understand, but I do. That's why you wanted to escape from me. A fine way to thank me, after you were screaming in there like a stuck pig!"

"Me?"

"Why were you screaming? Tell me, right here! Tell me, don't be afraid!"

"You were torturing me, without pity."

"That's right, say it! You're one of the new ones. Me too, I confess it without beating around the bush. You'll have to declare everything, even to what you just finished telling me: 'You were torturing me, without pity.' That will prove the bad quality of the anesthesia. Remember too the loudspeaker they set up to save themselves, that was not to keep anyone from hearing you. Those are just lies. That's what has to be said: it was low-grade anesthesia."

"Will they pass Cuelles?"

"Of course they will! Minister's nephew. And that's just another argument we will produce before the notary. But first we have to get ourselves in agreement. We have to bring Cuelles down, and the President, and the Recording Secretary."

"I noticed that they didn't like you a bit. And do you think that with your petition they will pass you?"

"It's my only chance."

They had come out on the street through a side door of the hospital. There they encountered Cireneo's supervisor, standing with the nurse dressed now in street clothes, with a splendid figure.

"Cireneo! Cireneo!" he called, gesturing with his hand for him to come nearer. "Don't you know this young lady?"

Cáceres had called a cab.

"Get in," he urged him. "Or will you allow yourself to be cajoled by that needle-and-thread nurse?"

Cireneo's supervisor kept beckoning, smiling and very persuasive, as if he were arguing with his rival over the prey.

"Come on, Mr. Suárez, let us take my car. Here it comes."

It was a magnificent automobile. The nurse got into it immediately.

"I can't. I'm worn out," Cireneo responded to both, and to no one.

"What do you mean, 'you can't'? We are going to the notary. Right after that, together with the lawyer, we will do the petition. It's necessary to get the upper hand on them, before they send the records with the verdict to the Committees."

In the neighboring buildings, some curious folk peeped from behind the curtains of the offices, others from the balconies. There were always some interesting scenes when the examinations were letting out.

Cireneo felt himself weakening. A wave of indignation mounted to his aching head, and he remembered he must go on home without delay.

"I'm not coming."

Benegas and Cáceres both remained perplexed.

"You'll lose her, you'll lose her," called out some who were standing at the hospital gate.

"I couldn't care less, I already told you. No one is going to move me from this spot."

"You'll lose her!" the nurse said to Teodoro Benegas. "He means to bribe him. Let's go."

Cireneo understood that this was not the end, but barely the beginning of something that had been plotted against him for a long time. He looked at Cáceres, infuriated. The latter saw that he was on the point of losing his last hope, that of involving the Faculty in a long lawsuit for his vindication. Cireneo opted to remain fast. He took out the print and set himself to scrutinize it, just to do something that no one could put in jeopardy. Suddenly his brain cleared. He understood with perfect clarity that nothing that had happened to him was absurd, but completely logical and in accord with his destiny. His whole life had been woven out of the fabric of an unyielding scheme, and what had happened to him this morning merely comprised the most resistant and concealed threads by which all the other days of his life were sustained. He found comfort in the still quite brilliant light of the firmament which seemed to enter into him through his painful wound and dissipate all doubt, all confusion from his mind. And, determined not to back down, while his supervisor and the nurse were calling from their luxurious automobile to draw him toward them, and Cáceres with his hand on the taxi's door was beckoning him in, confident that Cireneo would accompany him on the new *via crucis* of an endless appeal, Cireneo was looking at the sky as though absentmindedly. He began to whistle and went out into the street, with the cross of adhesive strips on his head.

THE DELUGE

No one believed that so many people would fit into that church nor that its naves were to be invaded by a horde of peaceful citizens, capable now of the greatest excesses. The fact is that, including babies at the breast, no fewer than one thousand two hundred persons were piled in there, sleeping on the ground, on the benches and at the base of the altars, preparing their meals on improvised stoves, satisfying the pressing needs of life with all naturalness, and abandoning themselves to extremes and excesses of promiscuity and desperation.

The interior of the church was still unfinished and the walls uncovered; panels, columns, socles all displayed like tissues stripped bare the bricks and rough construction material that was soon to have disappeared beneath marble and stucco. Scaffolding was still leaning against the walls and one could see that the work had been interrupted in an unexpected manner.

Nevertheless, the images were set up in their niches and on their pedestals, and the installation of the immense organ was complete; it took up the whole face of the wall, while a railing of chiselled and exquisitely wrought cedar closed off the choir loft. The colossal silvered pipes glittered with a resemblance to the enormous tapers of an apocalyptic candelabra. The main altar and the pulpit were also finished. Mass had been celebrated since the preceding year, and in that pulpit Father Demetrio on numberless occasions had complained of the weak and lukewarm faith of the inhabitants of General Estévez. On Sundays it was impossible for him to gather more than fifty persons together, and they were always the same ones. Now the entire town was there, along with whatever they had been able to carry with them, heaped together, out of necessity sheltered beneath the triple and enormous arched vault of the church, just as the priest in a fit of anger had one day foretold—that is, driven there by a disaster of Biblical grandeur.

Scenes from the life of Saint Julian adorned the stained glass windows, illuminated by the tenuous light from without; it was to him that the church, large and sumptuous as a cathedral, was consecrated. But everything else was hideous. Complete families formed little encampments, separated among themselves by curtains made of blankets or sheets stretched from ropes or wires that were utilized for drying clothes. The smoke from the braziers and the tobacco, together with the fumes from the cooking-pots and from the still-damp clothing they were wearing formed a dense atmosphere that pressed down on the breast, quite different from the angelic cloud of incense that was usually burnt there, in addition to the ceremonies, to mitigate the acridness of the emanations from so many beings and things pressed together.

For a week they had been there, sheltered from the flood which had almost completely covered the town. The water formed an immense lake, and no birds were to be seen, not even near the church. After a drought of three months, which had obliged them to remove their stock a long distance away, the Largo River overflowed its banks as had not been heard of for fifty years. After three days of diluvial rain it left its channel and poured into the lower ground, where the town was standing. In the distance were to be seen roofs, windmill derricks, treetops, and pieces of wood and floating household goods.

The citizens fled terrified, on foot, transporting in carts and carriages whatever they could load up in their haste. No fewer than sixty vehicles laden with provisions, clothing, and victuals of every sort. Only the wheels and the hardware of many of these remained, because they pulled the wood out in order to make fires. The horses grazed loose, without wandering very far from the carts, under which the dogs took refuge in the severest of the downpours.

As the caravan began arriving at the church, Father Demetrio became rattled. He tried in vain to prevent the fugitives from taking asylum in it. At the beginning they begged him with humility, and in the end they insisted. Under the drizzle that was falling slowly, unyieldingly, men and women began to bellow with equal ferocity. Father Demetrio, an old man of seventy years, and the sacristan, don Pedro, older yet, decided to open the doors a crack. The old priest had the impression of a mass desecration, as if the mob would run their mud-covered heavy shoes over his body and over the sacred religious objects. The avalanche penetrated and was occupying the free spaces, each according to the importance he attributed to himself. The principal families were installed in the sacristy, next to the main altar, or in the choir loft; the humblest in the side aisles. Apart or together, the citizens of General Estévez preserved unharmed their old ill-will, their rivalries and scornfulness. For that reason they found themselves in very embarrassing situations when for urgent reasons they had to direct a word to those whom they had denied any greeting at all to for years. The waters had invaded all their houses alike, and the same instinct for preservation had brought them together without reconciling them. Others, on the other hand, resumed contacts, especially the women. And since the days and the nights were interminable, they even set about a second friendship.

The church had been constructed on a hillock three kilometers from General Estévez going toward Felipe Arana, which lay fifteen miles off, more or less. At his death as an octogenarian, don Julian Fernández left a legacy of his whole fortune so that the church could be raised up there. It cost two million pesos, and for its support he assigned the interest on another million, deposited in certificates. It was there, right there, on returning from a trip, that he received unmistakable proof of his patron saint's protection. When his horses ran away with his light carriage and smashed it up and were killed themselves, he came out of it unscathed. No one understood the event except as a miracle, and without intending it, little by little he too mingled it with omens and subsequent dreams that confirmed him in his belief that it was indeed so.

In order to build the church, begun five years previously, it was necessary to bring everything from Buenos Aires: materials and workmen. The consignments of people and things occupied the rail lines almost completely during that period, and carload after carload of materials still continued to arrive. Engineers, architects, artists and artisans remained dedicated to the work with a species of blind devotion. There were masons of every sort of specialty, carpenters, locksmiths, painters, tile workers, a world of people constantly in motion, like ants. At the beginning it was thought they never would be finished with all that was projected; now it was done, and in three years more it would sparkle like a jewel in the loneliness of the plain.

This invasion of beings that seemed to have lost both shame and reason was viewed by the priest as a punishment from heaven and the natural result of the sins of incontinence that everyone knew very well the testator had committed. The very first day Father Demetrio fell into a state of anguish and he remained in his room, on his knees, praying. When don Pedro offered him breakfast, he did not answer. He broke into sobs and mutilated phrases in Latin which might as well have been fragments of prayers as invectives worthy of the prophets. Don Pedro did not succeed in understanding this state of depression, for he was accustomed to seeing the priest as rather cheerful and grateful to the Lord throughout even the most insignificant events. He had known him for a great many years, twenty at least, ever since he used to wander from one town to another with his peddler's pack. One fine day he reconciled himself to the peace and tranquility of ecclesiastical life, little dreaming that from their humble chapel the two of them would go to reside in a church that everyone would marvel at in astonishment. Father Demetrio had received him with all good grace, though as the years went on, since don Pedro considered Father Demetrio's fervor to be excessive on some days, scruples began to overtake him, and that ancient, never understood life as a solitary wanderer came back into his memory. But apostles and saints there were who had done the same, and therefore Father Demetrio could never decide to let him go, not even during those other times when it was indubitable that the devils were ruining his disposition. They tolerated each other indulgently, convinced that they could live together without any sort of affection. No one became congenial with them, and least of all with Father Demetrio, because of his irritable and unsociable character. The consequence was that very few men attended the church except for funerals and other ceremonies and pageantry, and the women considered the duty of hearing Mass on Sundays as one of their inescapable domestic offices.

Now their misfortune had obliged them to request that he shelter them there for who knows how long, and to stay together, friends or enemies, as in a common house.

They had brought provisions throughout the week just past, especially biscuits, and the cart returned empty to Felipe Arana. He could not succeed in getting even one family to decide to leave when they might have been able to, such was their confidence that it would soon stop raining. And now they could neither move nor get food, because the roads, and especially the Largo River, which ran between them and the closest towns and which it was necessary to ford, made it impossible. Once the few milk cows, all that remained of the flocks, were consumed, they sacrificed the greater part of the herd of horses they had brought, and soon they would have to kill the remainder. Although the rain had stopped two days previously, the sky remained clouded, and occasionally there was heard some far-off and prolonged thunder that seemed to break out in another sky separated from the earth by the thick mantle of clouds.

During the first days, Father Demetrio only entered the church on rare occasions. One morning alone did he say Mass, and then he did not receive the respect that was due. Many people were talking out loud and others were scolding their children. The youngest ones were screaming and crying, and the tumult increased, threatening to turn the holy offering into a pantomime. Even the priest had the feeling of carrying out a meaningless sham of a performance, yet he went on until the end. He gave the blessing and left, determined not to repeat so useless a spiritual assistance.

As it happened by coincidence that during the Mass the rain grew stronger with a furious impetus, the atheists attributed the cause of this calamity to Father Demetrio, rather in fun at first but eventually taking it seriously. He forgot that mortification on the following days and frequented the aisles, moved by charity, by curiosity, and by the desire to confirm the degree of destruction his guests were doing to the pews and the other installations. Without warning he would pull back the curtains and stand there before the scene facing him, without a word, always unexpectedly, or he would respond with some laconic phrase of reproach instead of consolation.

"This little boy is feverish, Father. Do you think he could be sick?"

"Boy with fever, table top with cookpot ring. Ask the doctor."

Along the aisles and between the pews and the altars the adults were crowded, squeezed together, most of them in shirt sleeves and nearly all shoeless. The shoes never succeeded in getting very dry, when they didn't end up shrinking, and it was a matter of constantly taking them off and putting them on again, for they went outside so often to look at the sky. A great many pews were piled on top of each other in order to leave more room free; others were accumulated against the walls by the entrance, where there were also planks for the scaffolding, boxes with paving tiles and slabs of marble. There they put to dry the wood they had pulled out of the carriages for firewood. The refugees pushed up close to Father Demetrio and persisted in talking to him, not so much because they needed soothing replies as because it seemed to them that he did not comport himself with sufficient solicitude and kindliness. The father admonished, sympathized, or fixed his glance on the breast of his interlocutor with the same remote indifference with which he used to observe them from the pulpit. On the third day of asylum, women and men began to mix, for until then they had remained, as they did during Mass, the one group to the right, the others on the left; and for the priest that was impudent proof of the fact that they had forgotten even the most basic scruples.

Outside were the dogs, trembling with the cold and plastered with mud up to the rib cage. There must have been two hundred of them under the rain, emaciated by hunger and humbled by the water. They would move around here and there, would all together break out into lugubrious howling at almost the same time; they would scratch at the walls and the doors with their claws, or get into fights without any reason. A number of them, injured by the teeth of others, continued growling defiantly after they had been hurt. They would seek protection in the most absurd places, on the abutments and the porches, against the foundation forms and in the remains of the dismantled carts, or they would stretch out with their heads between their paws, mulling over their abandonment. As soon as they thought they heard a familiar voice they stood up and began to bark or to howl again, re-initiating the habitual race about the church. They ended by taking on a certain lead-colored look, and those that died were not thinner than the living. They gave off a stench that seemed to penetrate the church, through its thick walls, because there was no other ventilation than through the sacristy, which gave on to the patio, and the odors that came in adhered to the things, to the bodies of the refugees, and remained in the atmosphere for a long time, cleaving to the mucous membranes of their noses. When the dogs broke into howling at night, the women answered from inside the church with prayers to ward off any untoward augury and the men with imprecations pronounced in more stentorian and clearer voices.

Among the refugees, and apart from them, were doña Ramona and her grandson Angel, the town beggars. The grandmother must have been about eighty years old, and the grandson twenty-one. But he acted like twelve at the most, because he had been attacked by typhus as a boy, and this was causing him to grow simple-minded, drawing him back toward infancy. He was too fat for the age he appeared to be, and his straight hair gave the impression of having often been wet and simply allowed to dry. He spoke very little, and appeared to see with his whole face, like the blind. As a child he had gone to the Jesuit school and was very intelligent, but the ravages of his illness were as noticeable in his mind as in his body. Grandmother and grandchild located themselves in a corner, between the piled up pews and the scaffolding planks. There they continued their beggar's life, almost indifferent to what was happening with them and the others. In the town the shops used to put aside the indispensable things they needed to live, but never money. So that they were just as before, more or less, sharing in the privations of the rest of the world. Next to them, also in the corner but behind a confessional, a foreign couple had installed themselves, Maria and Bronislav, with their six month-old baby. They were Hungarians but in the town they were known as "the Russians." They had arrived two years previously, and he worked as a bread distributor.

Doña Ernestina, the carpenter's wife, wept for the loss of her barnyard fowls that she thought she recognized floating in the immense lake among the heterogeneous objects that drifted about without stirring.

One would not have believed that a town so small and apparently uninhabited might have held so many people. It was suspected that numberless strangers were there whom no one had ever seen before, come there perhaps to augment their tributions and misgivings. With the close contact to which all were obliged, however, they confirmed who they were and the length of time of their residence in the town. In the end, the general impression was that everyone was either known or detested since some time long in the past. Among them, in a corner of the transept, was sheltered a Spanish doctor whom the local authorities had permitted to exercise his profession without renewing his license. He was respected because he attended the sick with an amiable assiduousness, not heeding whether he had to keep vigil with them the whole night through when the situation required it, and because he was moderate in his fees. He was conscious of his responsibility and proud of his profession. It was an elegant habit of his, always so correctly dressed, to hold his cigarette with three fingers while he was speaking, as if he were offering it to the one with whom he was conversing. The balls of his fingers were colored with nicotine.

The little that doña Ernestina's husband ever said always had to do with the kinds of wood used in the church, the hand work and rough framing, stair-steps and scaffolds, since carving and inlay work interested him but little. With that in mind he talked of his tools and the lumber in his shop, which doubtless must have been washed away over the fencetops or were rusting in their boxes. His conversation with his wife revolved about such topics, and if it had not been for the fact that the general affliction had more than enough importance to go around, he would have described in detail what all that meant for him.

In contrast to doña Ernestina's docile character, the wife of the station chief was constantly ill-humored, as if she knew that the one to blame for this calamity was her husband and she could not find the means of telling him so. In general it was the women who were bothered the most. They had to attend to their daily tasks as usual, though with fewer conveniences and whenever their husbands demanded, for the latter never took into account the circumstances they found themselves in nor showed any consideration at all.

They began to be worried over the scarcity of provisions, now tightly rationed and spoiled by the dampness, and their approaching depletion was predicted. They sacrificed the cattle yielded by the small neighboring farms, and nearly all the horses.

"Food is getting scarce," someone ventured, "We'll have to butcher the dogs soon."

"The dogs are going to eat us up."

Going out to look in the direction of Felipe Arana was transformed into a habit despite the fact that they knew very well no aid could reach them from that wretched little town. But where from then, if not from there? From Jagüel Viejo? That was seventy-five miles away. Finally their gazes were lifted from the miry roads and from the lake that had buried their town to peruse the always dark sky. To the left from the church toward the inundated village was the cemetery, encircled by an unwhitewashed brick wall. The angels loomed up, each one exactly the same, and also the arched pinnacles of the mausoleums. From the church they managed to make out the crosses above the surface of the water.

The station chief preserved his phlegmatic importance. He suffered from intermittent migraines that obliged him to remain stretched flat for hours and hours with compresses that enveloped his brow and eyes. When not prostrated by the pain, he would go out even though it was drizzling to contemplate the vast submerged plain and to breathe the pure air. But it was impossible to remain outside for long, either because the suspension of the rains never lasted or because the dogs would throw themselves upon anyone who came out, putting their smeared paws all over them, imploring, ferocious. Two days before, a horse had been killed for them and without waiting for it to be butchered they were tearing off enormous pieces which they bolted down hurriedly, attacking and biting at each other at the same time.

It was becoming more and more difficult to open the doors, for the dogs persisted in trying to get in, pursued by hunger and the bad weather. They had by this time devoured the hides and the bones of the horses and even the cadavers of their companions, which for some time had been respected. They barked, they howled, they scratched desperately in the mud impregnated with blood as if they once had hidden their prey there but did not recollect exactly where. As they whirled around the church they kept beating up the mud in a quiet maelstrom until it formed a pathway of muck smooth as a racetrack.

Father Demetrio came through the aisles and was surrounded by the multitudes that perhaps hoped for any kind of miracle from him, or for some news that might give them encouragement. He himself felt his own guilt in his powerlessness to render assistance to anyone in their misfortune, his not having anything to say to them, and his want of courage to invoke the righteousness of faith in that critical moment.

"Noah's flood lasted longer, for it lasted forty days," he said.

The idiot, Angel, who was listening attentively to every sentence of the old priest, replied with unaccustomed vehemence, "Forty days and forty nights, until the Lord got rid of all the sinners."

"Forty days!" exclaimed doña Earnestina. "We've been here for twelve. I wonder if the Flood is coming back!"

"If so, it's for good reason," answered the priest. "Get your child out of that pew. He is making it filthy and ruining the whole church."

"Father, do you think this could be a punishment from God?"

"They've even stolen the altar candles. See? That one there is from the altar!"

"We have to have some light. You can hardly see anything even during the day."

"The dampness ruins the matches."

"We have to put on our clothing when it's still damp."

"But for smoking and for filling the church with obnoxious smells there are matches enough to go around!"

"At nighttime we don't have anything for light."

"At night you're supposed to sleep and not do those scandalous things that you do, nor behave yourself like pigs instead of like Christians."

"Between the screaming of the children and the howling of the dogs, we're going to go crazy, if you don't help us."

"There is always some child that forgets himself in the night. You see how we are, Father."

"Why did you crowd yourselves in here anyway? This is the Lord's house. Look at the floor.... Stepping all over what's left of the meal...."

"It's a bone."

"Not even the potato peelings have been thrown outside."

"Father Demetrio, would you have a little alcohol? Rafaela has the colic."

"Let the doctor see her."

Behind the priest went don Pedro, not answering those who were interrogating him, with a certain solemn conviction that he also had come to be an important person. The people were crowding around, and he was afraid they would finally decide to assault the two of them.

"Father, you might do something for us," an old woman cried out.

"He is a sinner! He is a sinner! He is a sinner!" the idiot broke in. "That's why God is punishing us all."

Father Demetrio was startled; he looked at him fixedly, with his gaze less firm and sure than that of his aggressor, and joined his hands together forcefully. It became silent, and everyone surrounded the priest as if they had wounded him to death. But no one spoke in his defense nor shoved his opponent aside.

"May God pardon you, for you are out of your senses." And the priest made the sign of the cross over him, nearly brushing against his face.

"You are a sinner against the Church and the Bible," Angel went on, and he began to make the sign of the cross toward the priest. The latter reacted in the same manner, and it seemed from the rapidity and ardor of their movements as though each was contending for the honor or seeing his adversary collapse, struck down by the hand of God.

"The day is coming when the anger of the Lord will manifest itself with horror."

"Out! Go outside with Satan! Let this stubborn lunatic outside!"

"He will make the teeth of the wicked to grind, and corrupted priests will atone for them and for their followers."

Father Demetrio was continuing with his exorcisms in Latin and moving backward in a difficult retreat. Many people had gotten themselves behind him and would not let him depart.

"He has Satan within him, Satan within him, that heretic pig."

"He can say that again," was heard from a woman in one of the wings of the nave.

"He wanted to throw us out of here like the dogs."

"He hid the candles to let us die in the dark."

"Yesterday he cursed all of us, because some boys got into his room."

"That's where he hides his food."

"What are you saying, you detestable rascal?" Father Demetrio bellowed, throwing himself upon the idiot, who had ceased speaking. Seizing him by the shoulders, he roared, "Vade retro!"

The idiot had suddenly changed his posture. With his beardless simpleton's face, eyes opened quite wide, he began to sob, without tears, staring fixedly at the priest, who was mumbling phrases in Latin, face red and bathed in sweat.

Without releasing the idiot, he looked first to one side and then the other, comprehending that he was absolutely without protectors, alone amidst a pack of human hounds. Someone who had climbed up into the choir loft whistled, and the sibilation crackled like a snake in the confines of the church. Someone else made a powerful offensive sound with the palm of his hand. Women and children were crying, everyone was talking, and from outside, when they heard the shouting, the dogs raised up a piteous howling. There were some who rebuked Father Demetrio and some who defended him. But don Pedro continued immutable, firm and silent as if he did not know what he was to do in such unusual circumstances. The tumult resounded from the arched vaults of the ceilings and the walls, rebounding and falling over the new uproar like waves upon the beach. The priest was led to the sacristy, his arm supported by don Pedro. In the church everyone was talking at once now, blaming the idiot who, protected by the old woman, seemed to be ignorant of what he had said. His grandmother shouted, while she ran her hand over his head, "Leave him alone! Leave him alone! Those were not his words, they were inspired!"

For a few seconds the refugees looked at each other as if they had been given a satisfactory explanation of the incident. Some pews behind, the station chief, with his cold water compresses on his forehead and eyes, remained stretched out and unmoving, every once in a while dipping his towel in a jar placed on the floor.

Several people went out to quiet the dogs down, but as it happened, the latter took advantage of some negligence and rushed in furiously, knocking down pews, belongings, and people with diabolic joy. When the doors were finally able to be shut, nearly all the dogs were within. They ran about barking, searching for their masters. They leaped over obstacles and, like arrows, ran through compartments formed by sheets and blankets. A new tumult began all over again, worse than the earlier one. With kicks they attacked the dogs, but these threw themselves down before their aggressors without caring if they were beings known to them or not. They licked children in the face and left their mud everywhere. Those that did not find their masters hid themselves beneath the pews or took refuge behind the scaffolding and the big chests, or went into the confessionals only to depart immediately with renewed energies. If anyone attempted to drive them off with sticks or by throwing things at them, they showed their teeth and would have used them had this chastisement been kept up. Very quickly they returned to their jubilant demonstrations, passing from fury to innocent rejoicing. They began to investigate things with hurried eagerness, to lick the cookingpots, to pry into suitcases and baskets; and they ended by throwing themselves upon them without anyone trying to hold them back.

It was drawing toward evening. The diffuse light entered softly through the stained glass windows, and the images glowed with a subdued brilliance in their golds and colored stones. Haze and smoke dimmed the vast, nebulous ceilings, veiling them with a dirty, grey fog, quite similar to that which sometimes covered the plain. So dense was the atmosphere that it seemed to make the profiles of the shining objects quiver. On the main altar, on both sides of the crucifix, burned two candles that were constantly renewed, since they were always withdrawn before being consumed completely. They were kept lit day and night as a quiet supplication that the rains might cease. The church remained inundated by a vague murmuring which gradually died down, impregnated by the odor of the wet dogs. That odor managed to predominate over everything else, acrid and prickling to the point of provoking nausea. After some moments silences formed, compact and abysmal. Immediately was heard, rising like a broad, dark wave, the murmur of contrite voices or the whisper of prayers or the discussion of the unbelievable events. They deplored the insult to the priest and were waiting to see him in order to ask his pardon in the name of the idiot. Many feared that the quarrel might bring on the death of the old woman, and it was not known where she had hidden.

Outside, the dogs that had been unable to come in barked without ceasing, circled the church in packs, and with paws and muzzles scraped at the doors and the walls.

"We have to throw these dogs out, or else kill them."

"Better to let the others in. They've been ten days out there beneath the rain."

In the end, the doors were opened, and they came inside.

To the surprise of everyone, the old priest was seen mounting the steps that led to the choir loft, with the fatigue of sorrow and old age. There he remained without moving for some minutes; afterward he knelt down to pray. All observed him with interest and respect; even with sympathy. Immediately he advanced toward the organ console, and unexpectedly there resounded throughout the church a profound, tremulous strain with somber and reverberant voices that were gradually soaring and being refined in a mystical flight until they reached the highest notes of the instrument and of the possibilities of human hearing. The music sounded then

as it never had been heard before, and the hands of the
performer were creating a canticle of heavenly anointing,
improvised beneath the painful emotions of the insult and of the
forgiveness. The sounds expunged what the voice of the
sacrilege had stained: from the images, the walls, the columns,
the reddened figures in the stained glass windows, hearts, and
objects—from all equally. The music stretched out over each
thing and each being like a balm, purifying the ambience of so
much noxious influence, so much sin, and overlaid a fine,
intense epithelium upon all that was dense and inert in the
murky light of the dusk.

Afterward all remained in shadow, hardly broken by the
quavering dazzle of the tapers on the main altar; and as the
sounds of the organ ceased, that compact silence, damp and
gloomy, was once more perceived. The images of the stained
glass windows, where the life of the holy Hospitaller was
chronicled, were scarcely able to be distinguished, and the rains
resumed their precipitation with new fury.

With voice quite muted, one woman said to another,
"Ernesto has a fever. His forehead burns to the touch. Do you
want to take his pulse?"

The other woman approached the boy stretched out on a
quilt, face up, and put her hand on his brow. A little way off a
voice was heard: "Wet this towel in the rain water and bring it
to me quickly."

"What is the matter?" asked the mother of the little boy.

"Here," answered the boy, touching his throat.

Doña Ernestina came up to them.

"Have you any aromatic vinegar?"

"For what?"

"He needs it."

"I didn't bring any medicine. Honey of roses, if you want
that."

"No one brought any medicines. I only brought a bottle of
iodine."

"I brought a bottle of syrup. Do you want it?"

Pallid, shaken, the doctor went from one compartment to
the next, passing beneath the curtains, examining the children.
He answered no questions. He only repeated, as if to himself:
"There are no supplies, there are no supplies. It's incredible."
Presently he was seen seated on the steps of one of the smaller
altars, head held between his hands. When the women came to
search for him, he mumbled, "I was already there, I was
already there" and he did not raise his eyes. He held his hands
to his throat as if something were bothering him. Afterward he
found his way to the sacristy, opening a path among the people

who in lowered voices seemed to blame him for all their misfortunes as they had formerly done the priest. He called to don Aniceto and gave him a slip of paper from his prescription book, urging him to depart on horseback and get to Jagüel Viejo. It was impossible to ford the Largo River in order to go to Felipe Arana. But even Jagüel Viejo was only a village with a railroad station and a few houses.

Above in the choir loft talking was heard. There were several men there who had withdrawn from the aisles in order to leave more room. The two tapers of the supplication burned with reddish flames, and other candles here and there lit up the bodies of persons and dogs stretched out on the floor. It was unusually warm. The wax images, scarcely illumined, seemed to be flickering and their cheeks inflamed with fever. The Christ on the main altar glistened from the dampness that impregnated everything as if he were entirely bathed in a perspiration which, with the blood from his face, ran down his shoulders, his breast, his glossy sides and sunken belly, along his thighs to his feet. The atmosphere pressed upon their throats; the glowing of the cigarettes rose, burned more vividly, and then fell again. One noticed the fatigued breathing of the old men and the children, like a feverish palpitation. The nights were worse than the days, infinitely longer and more desolate, although no scenes of despair and anger took place.

So passed the night. The rains slackened.

The two Hungarians, Maria and Bronislav, were awake, with their daughter between them. She had died while the priest, the idiot, and everyone else were in the midst of their disturbances. From time to time the mother poured a small spoonful of very sweetened tea into the open mouth of the infant. The parents did not speak, and they had locked themselves together with their daughter in between, hiding her. The mother wrapped her in a blanket and there they had been the whole night through without saying a word. There was a great deal of excitement, though noiseless. Women and men were moving from one place to another restlessly.

By the following morning two infants had died. That day they also had to bury the doctor, a little way off from the children. They had found him lying behind the main altar, with his scalpel between his fingers as if he were holding a bloodstained cigarette. All were buried near the church, where the dogs had been digging to bury the remains of their food. At a depth of about three feet the earth was nearly dry. They buried them without coffins, the children shrouded in their little garments, the same ones they normally used.

Father Demetrio mounted the pulpit. All were subdued, expecting a lengthy sermon of reproach or consolation.

"My children: God tests us until the end."

It was the only thing he said, and then he covered his face with his hands. He was sobbing. Angel watched him with his fixed, mild gaze from his corner by the scaffolding. He wanted to speak but he could only babble incoherent words, hardly abusive. The old woman was repeating mechanically, "If he has to speak, he'll speak." But the idiot only succeeded in moving his lower jaw as if he were under the hypnotic influence of the figure of Father Demetrio, who still remained in the pulpit, covering his face. Afterward the priest got ready to descend, hesitantly. The people spoke with voices lowered; words and sobbing were smothered in kerchiefs and hands. The dogs sniffed about constantly, coming and going excitedly. With a weak voice, Father Demetrio begged them, as he was coming down the stairway from the pulpit, "My children: it is necessary to clear the church of the dogs. This is a punishment of God for the new desecration of his house."

Everyone looked at each other in amazement. Outside, just recently covered up, were the burial places of the children buried hours before. A shudder ran through the bodies of the women. The boys especially were trying to seize their dogs, or those they had closest to them, so they would not be thrown out. The Hungarians remained in the same place, seated without talking, preserving the same posture as before. They answered anyone who came near them in a laconic manner, and no one noticed that the mother did not have her little daughter in her arms.

The day was slipping past slowly, like light being extinguished with infinite listlessness. As night was coming on, the grandmother of the idiot was heard: "He wants to prophesy, he wants to prophesy!"

Angel began to walk determinedly, pulling his grandmother along by the hand. They did not want to allow him to proceed to the stairway leading to the pulpit.

"Jehovah's curse upon the sinners..." the boy said, and his beardless lip let these words fall from his mouth like a mouthful of bitter pap. But upon coming before the main altar, he saw the priest, who was rising to his feet after praying, and he stopped, petrified.

"He's going to speak, he's going to speak!" exclaimed the old woman who was now pulling her grandson, stiff and numbed, by the hand.

The dogs continued their incessant searching, by now familiar with the whole church, the stairways, the sacristy, and the interior rooms.

That night passed also.

The following morning, before dawn, many of the men were outside the church, looking in the direction of Felipe Arana and Jagüel Viejo to see if they could see any help coming. They knew perfectly well that it was not possible to get through on that road except on horseback. But don Aniceto might still bring the serum and medicines, provided they had them there. Nothing was seen in the heavens over the lakes, larger and larger all the time, except some gulls and solitary birds far away near the trees covered by the waters. The gulls were flying high above the church, from horizon to horizon.

The two Hungarians, still seated, had no fewer than fifty dogs about them. Without moving nor speaking, they tried to drive them away just with their bare feet. They would hardly move when the dogs would draw back, only to approach them again, quietly, stretching their heads out toward them. Between husband and wife was the bundle, now enormous, formed from all the blankets they had. They used them to wrap the little body of their daughter because they didn't want to let her be buried like the other infants.

Suddenly the sky began to clear and it seemed that toward the east a blue fringe was opening up against the earth, the precursor of the end of that deluge. They took advantage of the truce to bury the children and three adults who had died the night before, among them doña Ernestina. The priest pronounced the responses, and when he returned inside the church he continued sprinkling whatever he found before him with the aspergill, as if it were intended for the ceremony itself, which was already over. When the task was finished, his eyes went toward Felipe Arana, toward the town of General Estévez beneath the waters, and vaguely toward Jagüel Viejo. No one was to be seen. Only the gulls, which continued their soaring flight from one horizon to the other. The sky, though less gloomy, did not nourish much hope.

"The Lord will hear us," said the priest when he went out, having gone over the whole church with the aspergill. "There won't be any more rain. Over there you can see it is clearing up."

"To the south and west the storm is still stationary."

"It was also like that three days ago."

They all reentered the church. Many had stayed within, near their children, assisting them however they could, helping them to breathe. Bronislav and Maria still remained as they had been for the two days past, surrounded by dogs. The odor of decomposing flesh began to be felt, more penetrating than the usual stench. Everyone followed the priest with their eyes. He was making his way to the main altar to pray aloud. The tapers continued to burn, and the images in the stained glass windows allowed the dim clarity of the afternoon to pass through better than ever at that time of day. Suddenly a youth entered, shouting in a precipitate burst of happiness, "The rainbow, the rainbow! It's not raining any more!"

Everyone made haste to get out of the church, and the priest began to walk, reeling and firm at the same time. He gazed at the sky to discern any sign of a rainbow.

"There, look. See?"

No one saw anything. They were hushed, poised in suspense, hoping rather for a miracle than for the most remote likely evidence. For a long time they were like this, without anyone daring to contradict the deluded messenger. The walls of the church were drying off in the breeze. Only threads of water were falling from the gargoyles high up. Suddenly there was heard, from very far away, from the depths of the sky toward the south, a peal of thunder that went rolling as broad as the whole of the firmament.

"God will produce the miracle of rescuing us and will not permit us to die this way."

In a little while, something more prominent within the vague opacity of the clouds, another roll of thunder resounded, swollen with shadows and moisture. The sky became denser, surely because night was falling; and immediately, just as when it had begun again after the three months of drought, the rain released its thick drops down over the raised faces.